TROUBLE IN SEABURY

SEABURY - BOOK 2

BETH RAIN

Copyright © 2021 by Beth Rain

Trouble in Seabury (Seabury: Book 2)

First Publication: 30th September, 2021

All rights reserved.

No part of this book may be reproduced in any form or by any electronic or mechanical means, including information storage and retrieval systems. Except for use in any review, the reproduction or utilization of this work, in whole or in part, in any form by any electronic, mechanical or other means now known or hereafter invented, is forbidden without the written permission of the publisher.

Published by Beth Rain. The author may be contacted by email on bethrainauthor@gmail.com

❦ Created with Vellum

CHAPTER 1

Kate peeped through the window of the taxi as it drew to a standstill and breathed a sigh of relief. The Sardine looked quiet. Although there was light spilling from behind the closed blinds, the outdoor tables had been moved inside and it didn't look like there were any customers lingering in the yard like they did some evenings after closing time. Good. This was one night she'd be grateful to slip inside quietly without her arrival becoming instant gossip-fodder.

'Thank you!' she said, leaning forward and handing the driver what felt like a small fortune. She grabbed her bag and quickly hopped out of the cab before he could add any more to her bill. If she'd been off on a jolly she wouldn't have minded so much but given that it had been such a miserable trip, it felt a bit like daylight robbery to cough up so much cash. It was her own fault really - several people had offered to pick her up from the train station in Plymouth, but she'd turned them all down. This was a trip she'd felt she had to face alone.

Even though it had stung, the cost of getting to London and back would have been a small price to pay if it had meant that her beloved Sardine was safe.

Kate let out a massive sigh as she watched the taxi drive off, slowly navigating the narrow, seafront road. She turned to stare sadly at the front of her cafe. Her home. She couldn't believe today had gone so badly wrong. She'd really thought that by the time she got back from London, everything would be sorted out and she'd be happy in the knowledge that The Sardine was safe. Sadly, she hadn't factored Tom into that particular equation.

The man was a first-class prick, and today had just ended up being a very expensive reminder of the many (*many!*) excellent reasons she was divorcing him in the first place.

Kate hauled her overnight bag more firmly onto her shoulder. All this could wait until she was safely back upstairs in her flat with a glass of wine in hand. She couldn't stand here staring at The Sardine all evening. She just needed to pop into the cafe, pick Stanley up from Ethel, and make sure nothing major had happened in the day and a half she'd been away.

This whole trip had been terrible timing. The new cake subscription box for October was launching in just a couple of days - with a record number of orders to fulfil. She'd felt terrible leaving Ethel, Sarah and Lou to run the place.

Lou was still pretty new, but just like Sarah, she'd fitted in instantly. She also happened to be a keen cyclist, and it had been music to Kate's ears when she'd declared that she was more than happy to step in and cover the rounds on Trixie, The Sardine's delivery tricycle, whenever Kate needed a break. Or whenever she was forced to travel to London for a mediation session with her stupid, soon-to-be ex-husband.

There was a tiny, secret part of Kate that felt immensely guilty about hiring Lou. What if Tom managed to get his way? What if she had to sell The Sardine to give him his half? She'd have to let Lou go . . . Ethel and Sarah too, come to that. Add into that little soup of misery the fact that she'd be homeless as well as losing her beloved business, and Kate felt a bit like she needed a damn good sob.

No. She wouldn't give in to that right now. All she needed was a Stanley cuddle. She'd loathed leaving him behind, but Stanley would have hated London, so he'd gone for a sleepover at Ethel's instead.

Kate sucked in a long, deep breath, filling her lungs with as much of Seabury's fresh, sea air as she could hold. She was home. She quickly made herself a promise that, no matter what happened with The Sardine, she'd find a way to stay in Seabury. She'd find a way to start again. Everything would be okay. Somehow.

Finally, she strode across the road and let herself into The Sardine - only to be met by an entire table full of people waiting for her.

'Hello, you lot!' she laughed in surprise. They'd clearly been camping out in the cafe awaiting her return for some time. The table was groaning with empty coffee cups and crumb covered plates.

'So-?' said Ethel, bustling over and somehow managing to take her coat, remove the bag from her shoulder and draw out a chair all in one fluid motion.

'So?' sighed Kate, sinking down gratefully.

'How did it go?' demanded Lionel, staring at her across the table.

'Don't keep us all waiting!' said Mike.

'Was it horrible?' said Charlie, earning himself a swat on top of the head from Ethel as she returned to the table.

'I . . .' Kate looked around at them all. She was incredibly grateful that they were here for her - but right now, all she really wanted was a coffee and-

'Where's Stanley?' she asked.

'On his way!' said Lou from her spot behind the counter. 'I think he's only just realised you're back!' she said with a grin. 'You look like you could do with a coffee?'

Kate nodded gratefully, then looked down with a smile as Stanley's huge head landed heavily in her lap.

'Hello beautiful boy,' she said, softly stroking his ears. 'Sorry I was gone so long.'

'He's been as good as gold,' said Ethel with a smile. 'Sarah popped in before she had to head off to college and took him for a nice long walk along the beach, and Mike took him out again about an hour ago.'

'Thank you,' said Kate, turning to smile at Mike.

'It was nothing,' he said, smiling back. 'Now - please, put us out of our misery!'

For a split second, Kate wished that she'd arranged to meet Ethel and Stanley up in her flat instead of down here. At least that way there wouldn't have been an entire welcoming committee waiting to interrogate her the minute she got back. She looked around and gave herself a little shake. They were only here because they cared about her so much.

'I'm afraid it didn't go to plan,' she sighed.

'What do you mean?' said Lionel, frowning at her. 'Did they not do the job properly?'

The last thing she wanted to do was re-live the mediation session with Tom, but right now, she couldn't see a way out.

'It wasn't the firm's fault,' said Kate, shaking her head. 'They were brilliant. Really professional. Tom just behaved like a toddler. He didn't bring all the financial paperwork he was supposed to, he stomped his foot at every available opportunity and basically acted like a brat. It was a waste of time and money, and now I'm going to have to go up again for another session because we didn't get to the bottom of what we're going to do about this place.'

'Did you manage to agree on anything?' asked Ethel.

Kate nodded, then added a shrug. 'Just the stuff that had already been agreed by the solicitors. Tom still wants half of The Sardine, and I completely refuse to back down. I mean - I'm already paying him flippin' spousal support because he's such a lazy little-'

'You're *what?!*' demanded Lionel.

'I know, I know. But it's not very much and it's only for a few years, and it's my fault that we didn't work out. I mean, I *did* leave him.'

Lionel shook his head. 'But that's not how this works! There's no *way* that should be going on. I think you need a new solicitor,' he growled.

Kate nodded. 'I might have to at this rate. The thing is Tom's adamant he's going to take me to court for The Sardine. It's like he's been watching too much daytime TV or something - he was playing some kind of "big baddie" role the whole time. The poor mediator didn't know what to do with him. It was embarrassing.'

'But surely the courts won't touch this?' said Lou from the kitchen.

Kate shrugged again. 'They certainly wouldn't without this mediation malarkey. You've got to prove that you've done this bit first. That's why I went up there. I thought we might be able to get ourselves sorted out without taking it that far, but he just kept saying *"I'll see you in court!"* like a bloody pantomime villain!'

'Does he even realise how much a court case would cost?' asked Mike quietly.

'I doubt it,' said Kate. 'He reckons he's going to make me pay for his share of the mediation by the time this is all over too.'

'Well, that's *definitely* not how it works,' said Lionel, his bushy silver eyebrows now positively bristling.

Kate picked up her coffee, took a sip and then promptly plonked it back down on the table. It was delicious, but she didn't have the energy for it right now. She didn't have the energy to think about Tom any longer either. She needed a shower, and then she needed to go to bed early and pretend this mess didn't even exist. She would think about solicitors and letters, court cases and divorces once she'd had a good, long sleep.

'You know,' said Charlie, 'I've got one of me feelings about all this. I reckon it'll all sort itself out. Just you wait.'

Kate smiled at him weakly. 'I really wish that was true.'

'Well, true or not Kate love, you've done what you can for now,' said Ethel kindly. 'You look like you need a rest. Perhaps a shower and a glass of wine? I've left you a shepherd's pie in the fridge, and then maybe you should go to bed early?'

All eyes around the table swivelled to stare at her,

and Kate nodded. 'Sorry, guys. I'm wiped. I'll fill you in a bit more when I've had a rest?'

She got to her feet and grabbed her coffee to take with her. 'Lou - are you okay to lock up for me if I disappear upstairs?'

'Go on, boss - get out of here! We've got this.'

Kate was just turning the key in the lock to let herself into her little flat above The Sardine when she felt someone watching her. She peered over her shoulder only to find Mike looking at her awkwardly.

'Hey,' he said with a smile. 'I know you've got Stanley, but I was wondering if you'd like some company - or if there's anything I can bring you? Takeaway? Fish and Chips? Wine?'

Kate smiled at him. 'Thanks Mike, that's so lovely of you but I'm good. I've got Ethel's shepherd's pie waiting for me, and I'll probably just crash out after that. Sorry!'

'Don't apologise!' said Mike quickly. 'I just realised that we rather ambushed you in there - but it's only because we . . . because we care?' he shrugged, looking awkward.

If Kate wasn't so knackered right now, the sight of Mike Pendle, businessman extraordinaire, scuffing the toe of his trainer into the ground and looking more like a shy teenager than a grown man would have melted her heart. As it was, all she could really focus on was the siren call of her pyjamas and the numbing effects of the bottle of red she'd stashed for the occasion.

'I know you care,' she said at last, as Stanley gave a little whine, waiting for her to hurry up and open the door so that he could trundle up the stairs and get into bed. 'Let's catch up properly when I'm more with it?'

'Sounds like a plan,' said Mike, smiling at her.

'Great. Tomorrow evening? At the lighthouse? Leftovers picnic?'

'It's a date!' said Mike. 'Have a good evening, Kate.'

'You too,' said Kate.

She stood and watched as he wandered towards the seafront, turning in the direction of North Beach rather than back towards The Sardine.

'It's a date?' she muttered to herself, finally opening the door and letting Stanley amble past her before closing it firmly behind them both. 'I like you, Mike Pendle, but right now - after everything that's happened - the last thing I want is a date!'

CHAPTER 2

'Morning boss!' grinned Lou as she bounced into the cafe. 'How're you doing this fine morning?'

'Much, much better for a sleep and a shower to wash all that London grime off!' she laughed, adding the last order to the stack already waiting to be loaded onto Trixie ready for her morning rounds.

'I know what you mean. It does something funny to your skin, that place. Still, I love it,' said Lou, taking off her long, red coat. 'Don't think I'd want to live there, though,' she added decidedly.

'I hated living there,' said Kate, scrunching up her nose.

'I didn't realise you had! I had you pegged for someone who never left Seabury unless forced - like yesterday.'

Kate let out a delighted laugh. 'Then you've got me

pegged just about right. But when I lost my dad I thought it'd help to have a complete change. Turns out I was just trying to run away from how much it flippin' hurt.'

'Did it work?' said Lou.

'Nope. I was back here within three months leaving a disgruntled, jilted husband behind me. It just added to the pile of trouble really.' Kate paused and shrugged. 'Still, I had Seabury to help me get through it.'

'And Stanley, of course,' laughed Lou, bending down to pet the big hairy bear who'd just wandered over to demand a treat from his new friend.

'Stanley turned up not long after I'd come back actually. We kind of saved each other,' said Kate, smiling as she watched Stanley munching happily on one of his biscuits.

'So, do you want me to do the delivery round again today?' asked Lou, as Kate fired up the Italian Stallion, ready for their customary early morning coffee fix.

Kate shook her head. 'Nah - I'm actually looking forward to the exercise for a change. After sitting for so long on a train, I think a bit of pedalling will do me good.'

'Okie dokie!' said Lou cheerfully. 'Offer's always there, though.'

'Thanks Lou - you're a saint.'

Lou grinned at her.

'Oh - did Sarah mention how she did on that last assignment when she popped in yesterday?' asked Kate.

Lou nodded. 'You know our girl, she aced it! She was quite modest but reading between the lines it sounds like her tutors are thrilled with her. Anyway, I'm sure she'll tell you all about it - she's due in this morning, isn't she?'

Kate nodded. 'She's going to go far, that one,' she said, totally unable to stop a proud smile from spreading across her face.

Helping Sarah to get into college was something Kate was incredibly proud of. It had been quite the battle to convince Mike to let his daughter follow her passion. All Sarah had wanted to do was study professional patisserie and confectionery at college, but Mike had been adamant that she should stay in school and take her A levels instead.

Sarah had worked hard in The Sardine all summer, doing her best to prove to her dad that her interest in all things baking wasn't just a whim. Eventually, with a little added nudging from Ethel, they'd managed to win Mike over with a compromise. Sarah was allowed to take the baking course provided she also studied business management alongside it.

Kate suspected that the whole issue had had rather a lot to do with added pressure being applied behind the scenes by Sienna, Sarah's mother - and Mike's ex - because as soon as he'd made the decision to let Sarah go to college, Mike had been incredibly supportive about the whole thing.

Kate didn't usually take against someone so

completely. It had always been in her nature to believe that there was some good to be found even in the most difficult of characters. Not Sienna though. She'd never actually met the woman, but Kate loathed her. The moment she'd caused injury to her darling Stanley by running them off the road during one of their delivery rounds, Sienna had earned herself a place on Kate's shit-list. It was quite an exclusive list - the only other person currently on there was Tom.

'You okay?' asked Lou, taking her fresh cup of coffee from Kate with a frown. 'You were all smiley two seconds ago but I swear I just heard you grinding your teeth.'

Kate rolled her eyes. 'Unfortunately, even fleeting thoughts of my ex tend to have that effect on me at the moment.'

'I know what you mean,' said Lou.

'Were you married before coming to Seabury?' asked Kate, curiously, taking a sip of her own coffee.

Lou had been with her for several weeks now, but she didn't tend to talk about herself much. She'd arrived in Seabury at the end of the summer holidays "looking for a new start" as she'd put it, and rented the cutest little place on the hill just below the allotments. She'd bounced into the cafe on her second day in town, and Kate had instantly known that she'd be the perfect fit for The Sardine.

'Nah,' said Lou. 'Not married, but I'd been with the

same guy for years. We lived together - but no kids, thank heavens!'

'What happened?' asked Kate.

'Younger model,' muttered Lou. 'I mean, I wouldn't mind . . . but it's such a cliché!'

'I'm really sorry,' said Kate.

Lou shrugged. 'His loss. If he can't see that spending his life with forty-two years worth of awesomeness is far better than babysitting a teenager, that's up to him.'

'*That* young?' asked Kate.

'His new bit? Yep - just nineteen. I'm sure she's a lovely girl, but there was no way I wanted to hang around and be compared to that all day, every day. As *if* there's any kind of comparison, anyway!' she smirked. 'I was *always* going to win that competition. Just wasn't fair on the poor lamb!'

Kate smiled at Lou. She didn't believe for one second that it had been as easy to deal with as she was making out right now, but she couldn't help but admire her attitude.

'Morning dearies!' came Ethel's cheery voice as a large pile of Tupperware walked through the door.

'You behind there, Ethel?' laughed Lou, rushing over to remove the top layer of boxes so that Ethel could see where she was going.

'Thank you, love!' she smiled. 'I was *that* worried I was going to drop the lot - it's getting really windy out there this morning!'

She popped the rest of the boxes on the counter and did her best to smooth her hair back into place.

'Well, Kate - I have to say you look a lot more human this morning!'

'Erm, thanks . . . I think?!' laughed Kate.

Lou snorted.

'You know what I mean,' tutted Ethel.

'Yep, I do,' said Kate, giving her a reassuring smile. 'Everything feels a lot better for a good night's sleep - mind you, it was a bit more like passing out rather than sleeping, I was that tired!'

'Did Mike manage to catch you before you disappeared upstairs?' asked Lou lightly, ignoring Ethel as she dug her in the ribs with her elbow.

'Yes, he did,' said Kate raising an eyebrow.

'Well, that's nice,' said Ethel blandly. 'At least you had a bit of company.'

Kate rolled her eyes and shook her head. 'He just asked if there was anything I needed and then headed off home.'

'What?' said Lou. 'No cosy little chat upstairs?'

'Honestly, you two are impossible!' laughed Kate. She could sense that they were nearing their favourite topic of conversation - why she wasn't dating Mike - and she really could do without it this morning.

'No, Lou,' she huffed. 'You saw what I was like - I was good for nothing last night. I just stuffed my face and then crawled into bed.'

'Shame,' pouted Lou.

'Not at all,' said Kate. 'Ethel's shepherd's pie was just what the doctor ordered. Thank you, by the way!'

'No problem, my love. I'm just sad it wasn't a meal for two.'

'Okay, you two, quit it!' laughed Kate, just as the bell above the door sounded again.

'Quit what?' demanded Sarah, bowling into the cafe and instantly dropping to her knees to give Stanley a cuddle. 'Morning fluff-hound,' she murmured into his fur.

'We were just talking about Kate and your dad,' said Ethel.

'Oooh!' squealed Sarah, causing Stanley to let out a little *wuff* of surprise. 'Are there developments? Have you two finally snogged? Can I be maid of honour?!'

'No, no and nope!' said Kate, covering her face with her hands. Honestly, these three would be the death of her!

'Aw - come on Kate, get a move on and ask him out already!' pouted Sarah. 'I'm totally shipping you two!'

'Shipping?!' demanded Ethel, looking confused.

'Yeah,' said Kate, 'I second that. Shipping? Explain!'

'Honestly, you two old fogeys!' laughed Lou, 'get with the program!'

'Exactly!' Sarah grinned at her. 'Shipping is when, like, you're totally into a couple. Like - my new friend Rhona at college is a total Harry Potter fanatic - and she ships Hermione and Harry!'

'As a couple?' said Lou, pulling a face.

Sarah grinned and nodded.

'Well, sorry to disappoint you,' smirked Kate, 'but I'm happy just the way things are, thanks.'

'What,' said Sarah, shooting her a sly look, 'him eyeballing you longingly and you pretending not to notice?'

'GAH! Look - we're both in the business community together - we're friends . . .'

'Friends with benefits,' chuckled Ethel.

Sarah gave a half horrified, half delighted squeak and Kate's jaw dropped.

'Do you even know what that means?' hooted Lou, wiping away tears of laughter.

'Shared picnics?' said Ethel innocently.

'I think you and I need to have a little chat about the birds and the bees,' said Sarah, laughing so hard that Stanley stuck his nose right in her face to check she was okay.

Kate was fighting the urge to join in. She crossed her arms and glared hard at her three troublesome members of staff. 'Ethel - please don't say that in front of anyone else, I'm begging you!'

Leaving them all guffawing in her wake, Kate grabbed the first pile of deliveries and took them out to the yard to get Trixie loaded up. The sooner she got out of the way, the sooner the others could set up for their first customers.

She hadn't expected the yard to remain as popular as it had been in the summer, but they were already in

October and it was still proving to be a hit - with locals and visitors alike. She'd managed to get the local sail-makers to create a beautiful cover for the space - which seemed to enhance the feeling of being outside near the sea, rather than making it feel enclosed. She'd also gone to town and purchased three outdoor heaters. She hadn't had to use them much yet, but she knew they'd come into their own very soon.

'Right Trix!' she said, patting the bright red handle-bars. 'Let's get ready and get out on the road - we've got a busy one today. At least I know you and Stanley won't give me a hard time about boys!'

'Who's been giving you a hard time about boys?'

Kate cringed. It was never great getting caught in the act of talking to your delivery tricycle, but considering the topic of this particular one-sided chat, things were shaping up to be even more embarrassing than usual.

'Morning Lionel,' she muttered, turning red-faced to greet him.

'Don't take any nonsense from those three trouble-makers you call staff,' he chuckled. 'I think they make each other worse when they're together.'

'Worse. Better. Depends on how you look at it,' sighed Kate, giving him a wry smile.

'Well, don't worry. I won't poke my nose in. It's none of my business why you and Mike aren't all loved up like you should be.'

'Lionel!'

'Okay, okay!'

'What brings you here so early in the morning anyway?' said Kate, desperately wanting to get off this topic of conversation.

'Well, I wanted to talk to you about your ex-husband and The Sardine.'

Kate flinched, suddenly wishing they were back on the previous topic. At least that didn't make her want to sob.

'Now, don't look at me like that,' he said, reaching out and giving her a gentle pat on the shoulder. 'It's just that I think I might be able to help.'

'Really?' asked Kate, her voice flat.

'Absolutely. Perhaps we could meet this evening after you've closed up for the day?'

Kate bit her lip. Damn. She either had to cancel on Mike or admit that she was otherwise engaged to Lionel.

'Erm . . . I can't tonight, sorry Lionel.'

'Of course, no problem. Hot date?' he asked with a grin.

Kate rolled her eyes. 'I'm meeting Mike for tea - but definitely *not* a hot date.'

'How nice,' said Lionel switching to an impressive poker face.

'Yeah. Erm. Any chance you could keep it to yourself though? Not sure I'll live it down with the coven in there otherwise,' she sighed, nodding at The Sardine.

'Mum's the word. And how about tomorrow

morning instead - before you open? It won't take too long.'

'Okay, thanks Lionel,' said Kate. 'Come up to the flat though - I think I'd prefer to keep all things *Tom* out of the cafe from now on.'

CHAPTER 3

'I've brought a treat for pudding!' said Kate, puffing a bit as she fought to get her breath back. Pedalling Trixie up the hill towards the lighthouse for the second time that day had almost proved to be more than her poor calves could handle. The minute she'd spotted Mike waiting for her on the far side of the old lighthouse - perched on a tartan picnic rug with two glasses of red wine poured and ready to go - she knew it had been worth it.

In fact, if she was being completely honest, she wasn't sure that her racing heart was entirely down to the steep hill. Mike was wearing a slouchy old pair of jeans and a cosy, soft grey sweater. For a fleeting moment, all she wanted to do was snuggle into the faded cashmere and feel his arms around her. She swallowed hard. Blimey, the constant jokes and wiggling eyebrows of Ethel, Lou and Sarah were definitely starting to wear off on her.

She took a second to lay her hand against the old stone side of the lighthouse, sending it a quick greeting as she did every time she came up here. It had nothing to do with the fact that she needed to calm herself down before she got too close to Mr Pendle! She took in a deep breath of the chilly evening air and watched Stanley trudging around the bushes, sticking his nose into them and checking the perimeter.

There. Calm. She was calm. She wasn't about to jump on the poor man. Nope. Not at all.

'Here,' she said, walking towards Mike at last and awkwardly passing him one of The Sardine's new cake subscription boxes.

'This month's new selection?' he asked, flipping open the lid and inhaling deeply.

Kate smiled and nodded. 'And just so we don't have any disagreements, I've pre-chopped them all in half.'

Mike laughed. 'Good thinking, girl wonder!'

The first time they'd shared one of the boxes, they'd had quite a heated scuffle over the carrot cup-cake which had resulted in rather a lot of icing ending up in her hair and all over his face.

Kate placed her basket onto the tartan rug and dropped down next to it, glad to finally sit down. Mike quickly grabbed the two wine glasses to save them from getting toppled by Stanley as he ambled over to join them.

'Here,' he said, handing one to her as soon as she'd made herself comfy. Then he reached out to ruffle Stanley's ears as he flopped onto the rug next to him. 'Hello, you.'

As Kate watched Mike smiling down at her already-snoozing dog, her heart did something funny in her chest.

Ah, crap. This wasn't good.

This was the exact same feeling she had to ward off every time she bumped into Mike, and it was getting harder and harder to do. She was a sucker when anyone fell for Stanley, and seeing Mike be so gentle with him meant even more because she knew just how scared he was of most dogs.

She could trace the moment things had started to get worse back to the grand opening of Mike's cafe, New York Froth, just a few weeks ago. She reckoned it was the sight of him in a suit that had done it. But then, if she was honest, his scruffy down-time look made her knees go all wobbly too.

Kate cleared her throat. She needed to get her mind off of how bloody good Mike looked. It wasn't helping matters that right now, his dark hair, threaded with little tufts of silver here and there, was flopped forward onto his forehead as he petted Stanley. She stomped hard on the temptation to reach out and brush the strands back off his face.

'Cheers,' she said, awkwardly, reaching out and clinking her glass against his.

'Cheers!' said Mike in surprise, straightening up and grinning at her. 'So - how're you doing today?' he asked after taking a swig of wine.

'Better than yesterday,' sighed Kate, staring out at the sea. 'I mean - I'm back home, and I haven't just spent hours cooped up with my ex, pointlessly arguing in circles - so yeah, definitely better than yesterday.' She gave him a rueful smile.

'I keep telling you, I know a great solicitor if you need-'

Kate shook her head. 'No. Thanks, but no. I'm fine.' She didn't quite know why, but she'd made a decision early on that she wasn't going to accept any help from Mike when it came to anything to do with Tom. It just felt . . . wrong.

For one thing, Mike was a business rival. Sure, things were more than amicable between them at the moment, but considering the issues she was having with Tom were all about whether she stood to lose The Sardine or not, turning to Mike for help just felt . . . wrong. There wasn't any other word for it. For another thing, something was telling her that it was a bad idea to get help in dealing with her ex from the guy she was pretty sure she was starting to fall for. Not that she was ever going to do anything about that, but still . . .

'You keep saying you're fine but-'

'Do you mind if we talk about something else?' she said, smiling gently at him. 'Anything else?'

'Of course. I get it. Sorry.' Mike grinned back at her and Kate let out a sigh of relief. She *knew* he wanted to make this all better for her, but right now the best way he could do that was to help her forget there was anything to worry about in the first place.

She quickly drew the tea towel off the top of the picnic basket and pulled out the food she'd hastily packed for them.

'Brie and grape or chicken?' she asked, waving two wrapped baguettes at him.

'Did you cut those in half too?' he asked hopefully.

She grinned and nodded.

'Thank goodness for that. Share?'

'You've got it!' she said, opening both packages and placing them between them on the rug.

'So,' he said, grabbing half of the brie and grape sandwich and taking a massive bite.

She waited while he chewed with his eyes closed and swallowed the mouthful with a groan of delight. Surely watching someone eat shouldn't be making her toes tingle? She gave herself a quick shake, trying to pull herself together.

'So?' she said, cursing herself when she heard a little quiver in her voice.

'I've got some Seabury-style gossip for you if you want to hear it?' he said, turning to her with a glint in his eye that had nothing to do with the last rays of the evening sunshine bouncing off the sea.

'Ooh!' she said in excitement. 'Spill!'

'Veronica's decided to take The Pebble Street Hotel upmarket.'

'Yeah right,' laughed Kate around a mouthful of chicken. 'I've heard that before. What's she going to do, add an extra egg-cup full of cereal to the guest breakfasts and charge them an extra tenner for the privilege?'

Mike shook his head. 'Better than that, she's decided to start holding wedding receptions!'

Kate snorted.

'I'm serious!' said Mike. 'She's updated her alcohol licence, and even has her first wedding booked in - apparently it's just a couple of weeks away.'

Kate stared at him, wide-eyed. 'Well, all I can say is that I feel sorry for the couple.'

'Aw. Poor Veronica!' chuckled Mike.

'But Mike - ignoring the fact that the hotel's not exactly wedding-ready - *imagine* having Veronica in charge of what's meant to be part of the happiest day of your life! Talk about an ill wind wafting around!'

'The hotel could be beautiful if it was properly maintained,' said Mike. 'Maybe she's turning over a new leaf? Maybe she's decided to live out her dream?'

'You think?' said Kate, suddenly feeling a bit bad.

Mike let out a gleeful hoot. 'No, I don't think! She's probably come to the conclusion that she can charge a fortune for a wedding and do it as cheaply as possible!'

Kate nodded. Sadly, that *did* sound a lot more like the Veronica they all knew and didn't love.

'Well, I wish her all the luck in the world with it,' she said.

'You do?' said Mike in surprise. 'Really?'

Kate nodded. 'For the bride and groom's sake, if nothing else.'

'Good point. Well, I've heard she's getting some work done on the place before then - so I guess she's taking it seriously,' said Mike, reaching down and grabbing another piece of baguette.

'Well, she won't be using anyone local!' said Kate.

'I'm guessing you'll be around there to read her the riot act like you did to me, then?' said Mike with a laugh.

'Nope. No point.'

'Ah, come on Kate, play fair. You gave me a roasting about that!'

'For good reason!' said Kate.

'Okay - yes - I guess I understand that better now . . . but it's only fair for you to light a fuse under old sourpuss too!'

Kate shook her head. 'No, I'm serious - there's literally no point. None of the local firms will work for her anymore. She owes them all money.'

'You're kidding me?'

'Nope, afraid not. The woman's notorious for nit-picking about jobs and then refusing to pay on the back of it.'

'But surely they chase it up and force her to cough up?'

Kate shook her head again. 'See, that's her superpower. She's such a royal pain in the arse that every single one of them gives up before extracting the cash. It's almost like they decide it's worth the loss of income just so that they don't have to deal with her anymore!'

Mike spluttered a laugh. 'Superpower? The woman's a crook!'

'Pretty much. But it means that there isn't a tradesperson around here who'll do anything for her. She'll have to go to Plymouth - or maybe even further by this point!'

'You know, I'd almost admire her if she wasn't so despicable!' laughed Mike.

Kate shook her head. 'What a way to live, though. I swear I've never seen her be cheerful about anything, and she's never got a good word to say about anyone.'

'Maybe having all those joyful weddings at the hotel will cheer her up a bit,' smirked Mike, taking a swig of wine.

'Hah! Maybe.' Kate glanced sideways at him. 'You know - it's something we threw into the mix when we were all coming up with ideas for The Sardine.'

'What, weddings?' asked Mike, looking interested.

Kate nodded. 'Catering the receptions using Trixie. I mean, it would have to be for people who were after something a bit different - maybe vintage themed, or looking for a quintessentially English afternoon tea. We thought it would be fun to rock up at the reception venue on Trix and dole out finger sandwiches, cream teas and lashings of ginger beer - or tea - or champers!' said Kate with a grin.

Mike nodded, his eyebrows still raised. 'You know, I can just imagine that! It'd be something really different, and you could tweak it to fit each wedding.'

'Exactly,' nodded Kate. 'But - luckily for me - Ethel sensibly suggested that perhaps starting one new venture at a time would be a good idea!' she chuckled, patting the top of this month's cake box.

'I *do* see where she's coming from,' said Mike, 'but keep revisiting those new ideas, Kate - you never know what might be the next big thing for your business.'

Kate grinned at him. She'd not known Mike that long, and you couldn't say their friendship had had the most auspicious of starts - but she was constantly surprised by how generous he was when it came to discussing ideas, sharing thoughts and generally being a really kind friend.

Uh oh, there were those warm, squishy thoughts again!

'So,' she said, hastily hunting around for a safe topic of conversation, 'how's Sarah doing with college?'

'You tell me?' chuckled Mike. 'I think you see her more than I do these days.'

Kate frowned across at him. 'Do you think it's too much? The hours at the cafe as well as college?'

Mike shook his head quickly. 'Honestly, when I do catch a glimpse of her over breakfast or just before we both head to bed, I swear I've never seen her this happy. From what I can tell, she's doing great at college and she adores being at The Sardine with you guys. She's learning so much.'

Kate smiled. 'She does seem to have a spring in her step, and she's got so much talent. At this rate, I'll end up making her a partner in the cake-box business! She's so full of ideas.'

Mike sighed. 'I know. I just wish . . .' he pulled a face and went quiet.

Kate glanced at him. He was frowning down at Stanley, slowly stroking his finger down the big bear's nose, clearly trying to work through something.

'What do you wish?' she prompted quietly.

Mike let out a long, slow breath. 'I wish I could get her mum to see how happy it's making her.'

'Sienna's not playing ball?' asked Kate, doing her best not to growl.

Mike shook his head. 'She's livid that I let her leave school without talking it through with her first. I'm dreading her saying something to Sarah. I don't want her to dent that kid's confidence any more than she already has.'

Kate laid her hand on Mike's arm, and he looked at her in surprise.

'Sarah seems to be doing okay. Seriously. She loves living with you and she adores her life at the moment.'

'I hope she loves living with me, but sometimes I wonder-'

'Trust me, she does. She tells us often enough!' laughed Kate.

'Really? She actually says that?' said Mike, a look of delight crossing his face.

'Oh yes. Amongst her other wonderful qualities, your daughter doesn't have much of a filter!' laughed Kate.

'You get to see such a different side of her,' he sighed. 'Don't get me wrong, I love the fact that she has you guys at The Sardine - I just wish she felt as comfortable chatting with me. She's still being careful with me - it's like this long-lasting hangover because I was so miserable when I was with Sienna. I hate the fact that Sarah lost so many years of being a carefree kid because she was stuck in the middle of it all.'

'She just wants you to be happy, and to make you proud of her,' said Kate gently.

'Well, the first part's coming along nicely, and she's definitely got that second one sorted.'

'Aw Mike!'

'Now - don't try to change the subject - what else has she told you with this missing filter of hers?'

Kate sniggered. 'You don't expect me to give up all our girly secrets do you?'

Mike shrugged. 'Fair enough.'

Kate grinned but secretly breathed a sigh of relief that he wasn't about to chase that particular rabbit.

Because the idea of telling him that Sarah couldn't stand her own mother didn't really appeal. Neither did she want to tell him that his own teenage daughter had declared that she was "shipping" the two of them. Talk about complicating things!

CHAPTER 4

'Morning Kate!' beamed Lionel as soon as she opened her door.

'Hi!' she yawned. 'Sorry, sorry. Come on in'

Lionel followed her up the stairs and into the cosy, light sitting room.

'Tea? Coffee?' she asked.

'Cup of tea would be wonderful if you don't mind?' he said, beaming at her.

Kate nodded and left him to greet Stanley - who was clearly very excited about having a visitor this early in the morning. She shuffled into the kitchen and flicked the kettle on - anything to buy a little bit of time before having to talk about the mess her life was in right now.

Her evening with Mike had proved to be exactly what she'd needed. They'd laughed and joked and gossiped, and it had all felt incredibly easy, as long as she firmly ignored the large, multicoloured elephant in the room - the fact that every time she looked at him, she wanted to kiss his face off.

Still, it had served to take her mind off of everything else, and all the good food, a glass of wine and tonnes of fresh air had meant she'd slept well for the first time in weeks. So well, in fact, that she'd really struggled to get herself out of bed and dressed in time to let Lionel in.

Part of her wished she hadn't agreed to this - but then, she owed it to The Sardine. Hell, she owed it to herself to do everything in her power to make sure that she didn't have to put her beloved life up for sale.

'Here you go,' she said, padding back into the living room and popping Lionel's mug down on a coaster.

'Thanks!' he smiled at her. 'You know, I didn't realise you'd bought so many of my original paintings!' he laughed, peering around at the walls, which were dotted with his stunning work - all depicting Seabury at its finest.

'I adore your work,' said Kate, following his gaze. 'And don't ask me to pick a favourite, because I've tried and it's completely impossible.'

'Well, it's a huge compliment,' he said, his voice sounding quite gruff.

Kate smiled at him. 'Have you always painted?'

Lionel was a bit of a mystery - no one really knew much about his history. There were plenty of rumours and guesswork going around Seabury, but she'd had first-hand experience of just how unreliable that could be!

He shook his head. 'Not always, no - but it's been my hobby for several decades now.'

'More than a hobby!' said Kate warmly. 'These paintings should be in galleries across the world!'

'You're too kind,' he chuckled in delight. 'But no - for me, they are my way of relaxing, of letting go of stress and making sense of the world.'

Kate nodded. Blimey, if only she could paint - that sounded *exactly* like what she needed right about now!

She glanced at Lionel. 'When did you start? I mean - were you living here, or . . . ?'

'I was living in London.' He let out a sigh. 'I was quite a high-powered lawyer at one point. Dealt with some pretty nasty stuff along the way. And that only seemed to get worse when I became a judge.'

'Wow!' said Kate. 'I had no idea that's what you were!'

'Well no,' said Lionel. 'It's not something I tend to talk about . . . or think about very often, come to that.'

'Oh - I'm sorry,' said Kate, instantly feeling bad.

Lionel just shook his head. 'Not for any particular reason other than it filled my entire life with some of the worst moments mankind has to offer. I hope I did my bit. That's all anyone can hope. But yes, the painting - capturing beauty and kindness and friendship - was a way of balancing things up a bit for me. Now that I'm retired - it's the side of things that I wanted to keep in my life!'

Kate smiled at him. 'As a fan - can I just say, thank heavens.'

Lionel grinned at her. 'Anyway - all that does rather lead me to why I'm here, dragging you out of bed at such an ungodly hour!'

'Right,' said Kate, suddenly feeling a bit nervous.

'Look. You don't have to tell me anything, agree to anything or do anything you don't want to do. But I think I can help.'

'With The Sardine?'

'With this whole mess your incompetent solicitor seems to have left you in,' he huffed.

'The divorce,' said Kate.

'The divorce,' nodded Lionel. 'Or lack of divorce, in this case. By the sounds of it, it should have been done, dusted and tied up with a bow by now!'

'Well, it's complicated . . .' said Kate.

'Do you mind if I ask you a few questions?' said Lionel, pulling a spiral notepad and fountain pen out of his jacket pocket.

'Of course not!' she said, even though a voice in her head was screaming the exact opposite.

'So - let me just say - as a retired judge, I cannot represent you, so this is advice as a friend, okay?'

Kate nodded. 'Understood.'

'The fact that I have several friends who are still practising solicitors - one of which owes me several favours - doesn't come into the equation right now,' he laughed.

Kate swallowed. She'd answer his questions, hear him out and see what he had to say - but she wasn't going to be taking handouts. It just wasn't the way she operated.

'So - how long were you married to Tom for before you returned to Seabury?'

'Three months,' said Kate, shifting awkwardly.

'And had you lived together before then?'

Kate shook her head. 'He stayed here some nights - but not often. Sometimes I stayed in the place he was renting nearby.'

'But you weren't actually living together - sharing bills, that kind of thing?'

Kate shook her head.

'And when you got married - who did the place in London belong to?'

'It's a rented place. Tom had been subletting it while he was down here. I moved in with him when we went back to London - and I covered all the rent for those three months - plus the following three months as I was leaving him in the lurch.'

Lionel blew out through his nose, sounding a bit like an irritated horse as he scribbled on his pad.

'I'm assuming the answer is "no", but do you have any children together?'

Kate shook her head, doing her best to suppress a shudder that appeared out of nowhere. It wasn't the idea of having kids she had an issue with - just the idea of having kids with *that* idiot.

'And do either of you have children from a previous relationship?'

'No,' said Kate. 'At least - I don't, and he never told me about any.'

'And why did you leave him? Was there any foul play on either side?'

Kate's heart sank, this was the bit that made her feel like a totally heartless bitch. 'No. He never cheated. Neither did I. I realised I didn't love him - I was just trying to escape my grief at losing my dad.'

She paused and swallowed the thick lump of emotion that had just lodged itself in her throat. She glanced at Lionel, but he was still jotting down notes on his pad. She took a deep breath before continuing. 'I needed to get away from Seabury - it felt like I was trapped here after dad died. It took me leaving and moving all the way to London to realise that this was *exactly* where I needed to be.'

'And Tom?'

'He was a distraction from my grief. I threw myself into the relationship in the hopes that I could forget how broken I was. Then, the entire time I was in London, he badgered me to sell The Sardine so that I could contribute more to our life together. He wanted a new car, he wanted our own place, he wanted to eat out all the time. The list of things he wanted was huge. Still is, by the look of it.'

'So you left,' said Lionel.

'I left and came straight back here. I filed for divorce as soon as I legally could. Tom countered it - he wanted to divorce *me* - for desertion.'

'Unusual,' muttered Lionel.

'I think it was a pride thing for him. Anyway - of course, I agreed - because that's basically what I did.'

'Just words on a form,' said Lionel. 'The reason shouldn't make any difference to proceedings after that.'

'I know. But that's why I've agreed to pay monthly spousal support for the next few years. It's my fault this has happened. I should never have agreed to get married in the first place.'

'And this is why I'd quite like to dismember whichever idiot you've been using as a solicitor,' said Lionel, his voice unusually grim. 'That shouldn't have been agreed at all.'

'But-'

'No buts, Kate. In the eyes of the law, this should have been very straightforward - what's known as a "short term marriage divorce" - and there are no children and no dependents to take into account.'

'But I just deserted him.'

'It doesn't matter. After such a short period, you should both be leaving the marriage in the same financial standing as when you went into it. You didn't buy a house together, or anything else by the sound of it?'

Kate shook her head. 'No. But I made my last

payment on this place while we were married, so technically-'

Lionel shook his head. 'He hasn't got a leg to stand on.'

'But he's taking me to court. That's why he's determined to mess up the mediation.'

'Kate - the courts would chuck this out in seconds. But if he's allowed to carry on and force everything to go that far, it'll cost you both a fortune for no reason!'

'Right,' muttered Kate. 'Just like the mediation.'

'No - not just like the mediation. That's nothing in comparison. We're talking thousands, here - possibly tens of thousands. Each.'

Kate could feel herself going pale. She couldn't afford that. Hell, by the sounds of things, if Tom got his way she'd end up having to put The Sardine on the market no matter what happened - just to cover legal proceedings.

'Kate - are you feeling quite well?'

She shook her head, looking guiltily back into Lionel's concerned eyes. 'Sorry. This has all been an absolute nightmare - and I had no idea that it's going to cost that much!'

'But it's not. That's what I'm telling you. I would say that Tom's solicitor is only pushing things this hard because yours hasn't been doing their job properly.'

'But-'

'But that's despicable? Yes. It is.'

'But what can I do? Mediation isn't working

because Tom's hell-bent on getting his hands on half of this place.'

'Take a breath. We can sort this out. The question is - will you let me pull in one of my favours? I swear old Philip would love nothing more than to sort this out for you.'

'I can't ask him to represent me in court for no fee!' spluttered Kate, now feeling decidedly sick.

'Represent you in court?' hooted Lionel. 'This won't go anywhere near court if he gets his hands on it. A properly worded letter or two and we'll have this all ironed out and your divorce will be sorted, you mark my words. And if I know Philip - which I do and have done for more than half a century - it'll be done in a way that'll make sure that it's final. No ongoing payments and *definitely* no chance that Tom will be able to crop up in the future, rattle his chains and demand anything else from you. How does that sound?'

Kate nodded, staring at Lionel with eyes full of unshed tears. How did that sound?

'Can I think about it?'

Lionel nodded. 'Of course.'

'It just . . . it's too much to ask of you. I can't . . .'

'It's nothing - and if it means you can put this all behind you and get on with your life, it's worth it!'

Kate shook her head. She didn't really know what to do. It sounded too good to be true and every fibre of her being wanted to say yes, but it was too much to ask.

'I promise I'll think about it,' she said, her voice cracking. 'Lionel - can I give you a hug?'

Lionel smiled at her gently. 'Here,' he said, getting slowly to his feet. He opened his arms and Kate got up and wrapped her arms around the old man's waist, willing herself not to cry into his shoulder. 'Just give me the nod, and we'll get this mess sorted out,' he said, patting her back gently. 'Just don't leave it too long.'

For a moment, Kate felt like she was a little girl again, being comforted by her old dad. She swallowed hard before pulling back from Lionel.

'Thank you for offering to help me,' she said, her voice wobbling.

'It's what friends do. And when you're friends with someone in Seabury - it means you're family.'

CHAPTER 5

After her chat with Lionel that morning, Kate's delivery round felt like just what the doctor ordered. For the second day running, she pedalled with determination up the hill out of Seabury towards her friend Paula's graphic design office where she always made her first stop.

As usual, Stanley was happily ensconced in the trailer, and she was glad of his quiet company. That was the amazing thing about her best friend - he was always there for her but never asked her difficult questions or teased her about men she had the hots for even though she shouldn't. Stanley's company was exactly what she needed this morning.

Before Kate reached the Graphika offices, she'd made the executive decision not to share the news about Lionel's offer of help until she'd decided what to do. Lionel's certainty that Tom didn't have a leg to stand on felt too good to be true after the months of worry.

Even so, for the first time since that letter from Tom's solicitor demanding that she sell The Sardine and split the proceeds - she felt a bubble of hope. She almost didn't dare to think too hard about it. If she accepted Lionel's help, maybe, just maybe, this whole thing would be over and she could get back to enjoying her life without the threat of this great loss hanging over her.

By the time she pulled into the Graphika car park and drew Trixie and her trailer to a halt in front of the glass-fronted building, Kate had a big smile on her face – which was definitely a good thing as Paula and several of her colleagues were already outside, eagerly awaiting her arrival and enjoying a bit of Autumn sunshine while they were at it.

'We could set our clocks by you!' laughed one of the guys - who Kate was pretty sure was called Greg. 'I don't know how you do it, pedalling Trixie around!'

Kate grinned at him and hurried around the back to let Stanley down so that he could make his usual rounds and give hugs to everyone who needed them. As soon as he hopped down, she watched him make a beeline straight for Paula.

The big bear plonked his furry behind down onto her posh shoes and leaned back against her legs, staring up at her. Paula grinned at him in delight and promptly lowered herself into a squat so that she could wrap her arms around him.

'I *am* honoured,' she laughed, 'but I know it's only because I've got one of your faves in my pocket!'

Kate watched as her friend drew out a Rich Tea biscuit, snapped it in half and fed a piece to Stanley. He took it from her gently and it was gone in seconds. He quickly resumed his leaning and ignored the proffered second half.

Kate did her best to hide her frown of concern. Stanley only tended to ignore food and glue himself to someone when he sensed they were worried, upset or poorly. She made a mental note to check in with Paula when she wasn't surrounded by her colleagues. She'd seemed a lot better recently after her strange bout of ill-health back in the summer - but Kate had learned to trust Stanley's intuition when it came to people needing a little bit of extra TLC.

'So,' said Greg, snapping her attention back to him, 'are this month's cake boxes ready?'

Kate couldn't help but smile at his boyish excitement as she nodded.

'Yep - I've got everyone's orders here, and the three boxes you ordered for the office too!'

There was a general cheer at this, and it made Kate's heart sing. She was so proud of what her little team had achieved in such a short time. This month's boxes had a special autumn theme - so there was plenty of orange icing, cinnamon and spiced flavours, and the most divine little pumpkin cake-pops that Sarah had designed, complete with a salted caramel centre.

Kate busied herself doling out sandwiches and cake boxes until everyone had what they'd ordered and had disappeared back inside, shouting their thanks to her. Kate turned to have a few words with Paula before setting off for her next stop, only to find her friend still sitting with her arms around Stanley.

'You two okay down there?' she smiled.

'Erm, yes . . . but I think my feet have gone to sleep. Your pooch is quite heavy!' laughed Paula. 'Give me a hand?'

Kate grinned at her friend as she reached both hands down to her. The strange feeling she'd had five minutes ago cleared as she hauled her, laughing, up from the pavement. Stanley clearly thought that his hug had done the business too as he quickly snaffled the second half of the biscuit that Paula had left on the pavement.

Paula leant on Kate's shoulder as she stomped her feet, desperately trying to get some feeling back into them.

'So,' she said, 'dare I ask how it went with Tom?'

Kate pulled a face. 'Even worse than we were joking about!' she muttered.

'Ah crap, I'm sorry. What'll you do next?'

Kate shrugged, suddenly feeling a bit bad about her decision to keep Lionel's offer of help to herself, but she stuck with it.

'I'll just have to wait and see what happens next, I guess. Tom's not known for being a man of fast and decisive action,' she said with a grim smile.

'Ain't that the truth!' muttered Paula, reaching out and giving her hand a squeeze. 'You okay?'

Kate smiled at her and nodded. 'Yes. I'm okay. I'm just going to focus on enjoying autumn in Seabury. The rest will just have to work itself out.'

Paula smiled at her. 'Sounds like a plan to me. And . . . dare I ask . . . any progress with Mike?'

Kate groaned. 'Not you too?! That's all I'm hearing at The Sardine at the moment!'

'Oops. Sorry,' said Paula, but Kate noticed that she was looking anything but sorry. 'Us old married types have to get our kicks somewhere!'

'You're not old,' said Kate, desperately clutching at straws to change the subject. 'Fifties are the new twenties!'

Paula snorted. 'Tell that to my knees! Anyway - I've been married to Ryan since the dawn of time. Let me live vicariously!'

'I would if there was anything to report - but there isn't. We're friends. We had a lovely picnic last night up at the lighthouse.'

'How romantic!' sighed Paula, clearly choosing to ignore the bits she didn't want to hear.

'Hardly! We just talked about our twattish exes and Seabury gossip.'

'Don't tell me you're not attracted to him,' said Paula, wiggling her eyebrows.

Kate went quiet and frowned at her friend for a minute. 'Okay, I won't,' she said at last, causing Paula to squeal with excitement. 'Seriously though - with everything going on with Tom, and The Sardine, and Mike's business just getting on its feet - this isn't the right time. It might never be the right time . . .'

'Never say never!' was Paula's infuriating reply as she grabbed her own cake box along with a baguette from Trixie's trailer. 'Sorry lovely, I need to get back inside - conference call coming up. Urgh. Whoever invented video calling should be shot.'

Kate laughed. 'Catch up soon?' she said.

'I'll be in with the Chilli Dippers on Wednesday morning. We do need a proper catch up over a glass of wine soon though!'

'Sounds perfect,' said Kate, opening the back of the trailer so that Stanley could hop back in. Paula gave him one last tickle behind the ears, kissed Kate on the cheek and then headed back into the office.

'You'll never guess who's staying in that holiday cottage that ordered the two cake boxes out of the blue,' said Kate, striding back into The Sardine after parking Trixie up outside.

'Who?' asked Ethel, instantly firing up the Italian

Stallion. 'And whoever it was, I hope you were nice to them young lady!' she frowned, making Lou chuckle over the teacakes she was busy laying out under the grill for toasting. 'I know you don't approve of second homes and all that, but paying customers are exactly what we need!'

Kate smirked. Ethel never would give up scolding her now and then when she was being stubborn about something.

'Of course I was nice!' she said. 'Actually, it was kind of hard not to be - they were so grateful for the treats. I don't think they've been having the best time.'

'Well,' said Lou, 'tell us. Who is it?'

'It's that couple who're holding their wedding reception in The Pebble Street Hotel in a couple of weeks,' said Kate. 'They've decided to rent that place until the wedding - a bit of a pre-wedding holiday so that they're close by!'

'How lovely!' said Ethel in surprise. 'But surely they should be having the time of their lives!'

Kate shook her head. 'Annabel - the bride-to-be - actually seemed quite down when she first answered the door. We got talking and I could tell she was trying to be a bit discreet and everything, but . . . reading between the lines, I'd say Veronica's already giving them the runaround!'

'Why doesn't that surprise me?!' huffed Ethel. 'There should be a law against that woman being allowed anywhere near someone's big day.'

Lou nodded. 'Yeah - she doesn't really seem the type that should be in that line of business, does she?'

'You've met her, then?' asked Kate, taking a coffee from Ethel and gratefully flopping down into one of the chairs for a moment while the cafe was quiet.

'Erm, yeah.'

Kate raised her eyebrows as a decidedly sheepish look crossed Lou's face.

'What's happened?' said Kate suspiciously.

'First of all - I'm really sorry, I didn't realise what she was like.'

'How could you, love?' said Ethel. 'You're new in town. I shouldn't have left you on your own for so long. It's my fault.'

'Alright you two, what's the wicked witch of Pebble Street been up to now?'

'Well, she came in when Ethel was having a chat with Charlie out in the yard. I told her to take a bit of a break, and Veronica came in.'

'In here?' said Kate in surprise. 'Blimey, that's the first time in months.'

'Yeah, well, we think she clocked that you and Ethel were both out of the way,' huffed Lou.

'So what's so bad?'

'She wangled a free coffee out of Lou for a start,' huffed Ethel. 'Told her you always ran a tab for her.'

Kate chuckled. 'She's incorrigible, you have to hand it to her.'

'I can think of ruder words that suit her better!' said Ethel.

'I did run a tab for her, years ago,' said Kate.

'Until we realised that she never ever coughs up,' said Ethel.

'Indeed,' said Kate raising a bemused eyebrow. 'So I'll just add another cappuccino to the dozens lost in that direction. Seriously Lou, don't worry about it. No big deal.'

'The coffee might not be, but-'

'Uh oh, this doesn't sound good!'

'That's because it's not,' scowled Ethel. Lou flinched and Ethel quickly patted her on the shoulder. 'Not you love - her!'

'She's ordered twenty-five cake boxes for that wedding,' said Lou quickly, like she was yanking off a plaster.

'Uh huh?' said Kate, a sinking sensation hitting her in the pit of her stomach.

'I asked her for payment upfront - like we've been doing all along - and she said that you always give her a fifty per cent discount for bulk orders for the hotel.'

Ethel let out a rumbling growl which was quickly echoed by a surprised Stanley.

'Sorry boy!' said Ethel, quickly feeding him a biscuit from her apron pocket to make up for scaring him.

'Oh. She did, did she?' said Kate.

Lou nodded. 'I'm really sorry.'

'She's paid for half already?' said Kate, mildly surprised.

'A cheque,' said Ethel shortly.

'Ah. She's back at that old game, is she?' said Kate lightly.

Lou nodded. 'Ethel told me they always bounce.'

'Always,' said Kate.

'I'm so sorry.'

'It's not your fault. I'll sort this one out - she was trying it on because you're new, that's all.'

'I can't believe she'd do that,' said Lou, looking hurt.

'Don't take it personally, love,' said Ethel. 'That old witch is an equal opportunity piss-taker.'

'Sadly, Ethel's right,' said Kate. 'And Lou - please don't worry! I should have told you about her, but she hasn't set foot in here for months, so I didn't really think about it.'

Lou nodded. 'Thanks Kate. And sorry.'

Kate just shook her head. 'Just for future reference - she has to pay for everything upfront when she orders - whether that's a coffee, breakfast or even a massive order for the hotel. But don't worry, I doubt you'll be seeing her in here again anyway. I'll be having words.' Kate paused and blew out a breath impatiently. 'In fact, I think I'll go pay her a visit right now. Pass me that cheque and keep an eye on Stanley for me!'

CHAPTER 6

Kate stomped along the seafront towards where The Pebble Street Hotel stood on the border of The Kings Nose - the grassy, rocky outcrop which speared out into the bay and separated West Beach from North Beach.

The hotel had been a really beautiful building in its heyday - it still was, if you could see past the peeling paint, windows that desperately needed repairing or replacing, and the general air of unkemptness that seemed to linger around it. It was a real shame that Veronica had let it get this scruffy - it was in a prominent position and could be a jewel in Seabury's crown if it was properly loved and looked after.

As Kate let herself into the narrow, weed-filled front garden, she wondered how Veronica had managed to bag herself the wedding booking in the first place with the hotel in such a state. The reception was due to take place in just a couple of weeks so it wasn't as though she had much time to get it spruced up before then. Not that Kate could believe the old skinflint was planning on spending a penny more than she had to on the event.

She paused at the front door, unsure for a moment whether she should knock or just wander straight in. She shrugged. If she were a guest, she'd just let herself in and head to reception, so she decided to do just that.

Turning the large brass knob, she pushed hard and found herself in the foyer. It had been years since she'd stepped foot in here - not since before her dad had passed away - and the sight of just how grubby and unloved the foyer looked made her quite sad. The parquet floor was still there, and would no doubt still be very beautiful if it was given a tiny bit of love and attention. As it was, it was filthy and didn't look like it had seen a mop in years - let alone any polish.

Over to the right stood a large oak reception desk, piled high with what looked to be an entire year's worth of paperwork, and at least several days' worth of old coffee cups. Kate wrinkled her nose and read the sign. Well, she *would* ring the bell for attention if she could see the bell, but she had a sneaking suspicion it had probably been covered up some time back in the spring - and it might take several hours of shifting papers around to unearth it.

Sod it - she'd have a little snoop around while she

was here and see if she could find Veronica while she was at it.

Ignoring the sweeping staircase with its moth-eaten carpet, Kate headed towards the back of the building where she knew the guest lounge and dining room lay. She peeped into the lounge first and wrinkled her nose again. It smelled a bit like old cabbage. The little tables still held the remains of guest breakfasts - though they didn't look like today's. Partially empty bowls with dregs of old milk and a few cornflakes that had been left to weld themselves onto the china lay scattered on the tables. Discarded paper towels littered the floor and several cups boasting the cold, scummy remains of un-drunk coffee lay abandoned here and there.

Kate drew back into the hallway and made her way through to the dining room instead. She had to admit, she'd had no idea how bad things really were in here. She hadn't really given much thought to how Veronica was managing, considering she had no staff left.

For a moment, Kate was overwhelmed by a wave of pity - but that promptly disappeared when she remembered that Veronica didn't have any staff because she never paid their wages on time - if ever - treated them appallingly, and had basically earned herself the title of Boss From Hell.

Kate wrapped her arms around herself, not really wanting to touch anything. It was all just so . . . grubby! Sure, she could still just about make out the forgotten splendour of the building buried under the layers of grime, but she couldn't for the life of her imagine why anyone would want to hold their wedding here!

Reaching the dining room, she let herself in. Ah. Okay, this might go some way to explaining it!

Mike had mentioned that Veronica was getting some work done on the place - and by the looks of things, she'd found that work in progress. The room had been newly painted in a soft, vintage eggshell. A couple of the windows had been re-glazed and it looked like there were new light fittings in the works too. The mangy carpet that was in evidence everywhere else had been removed, and she could see that certain parts of the parquet had already been beautifully restored.

'Can I help you?' asked a guy who was on his hands and knees, clearly hard at work in the far corner, laying a new section of floor with painstaking precision.

'Oh hi!' she smiled. 'This looks amazing!'

'Thank you. These old floors are a bit of a labour of love, but so worth it. I'm sorry, though - this room is closed to guests at the moment. We're doing it up for a wedding in a few weeks.'

Kate nodded. 'Yeah, sorry - I'm not a guest - I was looking for Veronica? It's about the ... erm ... catering for the wedding,' she invented quickly. Well, it was *kind* of true, wasn't it?

'Oh. Well, she went to get me a cup of coffee about an hour ago,' he said with a rueful smile. 'Between you and me though, the one she brought me yesterday was foul so I'm not too bothered!'

Kate laughed. 'Do you get a lunch break?' she asked.

The guy nodded. 'I'm pretty sure she'd quite like me to work straight through, but a man's got to eat! I asked my wife to pack something for me today though - Veronica's sandwiches have proven themselves to be . . . inedible?' he chuckled.

'Tell you what,' said Kate, instantly taking pity on the poor man, 'why don't you pop over to my cafe when you stop for your break? I'll treat you to lunch on the house!'

'You don't need to do that,' said the guy with a shy smile.

'It'd be my pleasure,' she said. 'I'm Kate, by the way.'

'Ken. And you've cheered me right up, Kate. Thank you!'

'I'm just a couple of minutes away, overlooking West Beach - at The Sardine?'

'I know it! I spotted it on my way in.'

'Great. See you for lunch, then. Right, I'd better go and hunt down Veronica.'

'Good luck!' he laughed.

Kate grinned at him and left him to it. She hated the fact that the poor guy was probably never going to see the money for such a huge job. She just hoped that he'd had the sense to get some of it paid upfront - but somehow she doubted it - that would be one of the reasons Veronica would have chosen him for the job in the first place.

Kate made her way back towards the kitchen, pushed at the swing door and was met with a screech.

'What on earth are *you* doing here?' demanded Veronica. She had a pair of rubber gloves on and was busy scraping mouldy food off of plates into a massive bucket - which looked like it hadn't been emptied in weeks.

Kate did her best to breathe through her mouth. The room smelled *bad*. Really, really *bad*. The kind of bad that a health and safety inspector would take one sniff of and have a fit.

'Can I have a word,' said Kate, doing her best not to choke. 'Maybe . . . not in here?'

'I don't have time,' said Veronica, curtly.

'It'll take thirty seconds.'

'Fine!' huffed Veronica, yanking her marigolds off with a double rubber snap and tossing them on top of the ginormous pile of washing up. 'Follow me.'

She pushed open a door that led out of the back of the building and Kate followed, hot on her heels, desperate for some fresher air.

'Wow!' she said, as soon as she'd escaped the stench. 'What a view!'

They were at the back of the hotel, overlooking The King's Nose and the sea beyond. Kate took a couple of steps away from the hotel and turned to peer around her. Over to her left was a beautiful, paved patio area that had obviously been newly cleared, cleaned down and repaired. The large flagstones were even and new sand was in evidence between them. There were even brand new planters around the edges of the space, with large sacks of compost standing ready in front of them. A set of glazed, double doors currently stood closed, but she'd bet anything that they led back into the dining room where Ken was busy at work.

'That looks amazing,' she said sincerely. 'What a beautiful space!'

Veronica snorted. 'A wedding reception with a sea view. That's a premium product. Idiots will pay through the nose for that.'

Kate bit her tongue. Of *course* Veronica wasn't one to see the romance in the place. She sighed. It was so, so sad that such a special place belonged to someone without the tiniest drop of magic in her soul. Ah well.

'Look, what do you want?' huffed Veronica. 'I've got a lot to do, and I don't trust that bloke not to rob me blind, neither.'

'What bloke?' said Kate in surprise. 'Do you mean Ken?'

'Ken? I don't know about that. The chippie in the dining room. Never trust a tradesman. All crooks,' she said.

Kate heaved a sigh. There really wasn't any point in arguing with Veronica - and yet-

'He seems like a lovely man,' she said stoutly. 'And he's doing a beautiful job on that floor.'

'Ruddy well should do too, the price he's charging.'

Kate raised her eyebrows. 'Well, it's specialist work.'

'It's a few bits of wood in some bleedin' holes,' grumbled Veronica.

'Well - you *are* going to pay him, fair and square, aren't you?'

Kate watched Veronica turn an interesting shade of puce and was suddenly very glad that they were outside. She could always make a hasty getaway onto The King's Nose if Veronica went supernova on her.

'What exactly are you insinuating?' she finally hissed.

'Oh nothing,' said Kate breezily. 'Anyway. Let's talk about why I came to see you. You wanted twenty cake boxes?'

'That's what I told the idiot you've got working for you. I've paid up too.'

'No, you haven't,' said Kate. 'You gave Lou a cheque. You *know* I don't accept cheques.'

Veronica shrugged. 'She said it was fine, so it's done now. You can't back out, we've got an agreement.'

Kate laughed. 'Veronica, we both know your cheques are made of rubber! Plus - it wouldn't be enough anyway. I don't know where you got the idea I'd give you a fifty per cent discount?'

'That was the girl!' said Veronica, crossing her arms. 'She offered. I'm not going to say no, am I? Anyway, you can't change your prices after the fact!'

Kate rolled her eyes and held the cheque up in front

of Veronica. She proceed to tear it into strips, then into little squares, until she had a pile of pieces in the palm of her hand.

'Here!' she said with a wide smile, holding her hand out.

Veronica instinctively reached out, and before she knew what was happening, Kate had poured the torn pieces of cheque into her open palm.

'I . . . you . . .!'

'There's your confetti sorted at least,' said Kate, fighting to keep her face straight. 'Now then - I'll be glad to make up the cake boxes for you, and I'll even happily offer you a ten per cent discount as a local business. But you'll need to pay in advance, in full, by the end of the week if you would like us to add your order to the book.'

'You can't . . .' spluttered Veronica.

'You can apologise to Lou while you're at it too.' Kate smiled sweetly at her then stepped back towards the hotel, preparing to hold her breath for the dash back through the kitchen. 'Oh,' she said, turning to Veronica one last time before making her escape, 'we take cash or card, your choice.'

CHAPTER 7

Kate was partway back towards The Sardine when she paused, changing her mind. Quickly whipping out her phone, she pulled up Lou's number and sent her a text, letting her know that she was nipping over to New York Froth to warn Mike not to take any shit from Veronica.

She could only imagine that he'd be next on her list - not that he did fresh cakes, but she wouldn't put it past Veronica to get him to bulk-order something just for her. She quickly added a note about making sure that if a guy called Ken came in before she got back, he was to be treated to the royal welcome as well as a hot drink and whatever he fancied for lunch.

I'll explain when I get back. K x

Kate quickly hit send, pocketed her phone and strode back in the opposite direction, making her way towards North Beach and the beautiful, newly opened New York Froth.

When she arrived, she paused briefly outside. How ridiculous - she had butterflies, and she knew they had nothing to do with warning Mike about Veronica. They were just about Mike himself. This crush - or *whatever* she had going on - was getting silly. In fact, it was time to get over it. Seabury was too small a town to avoid someone, and besides, she didn't want to avoid Mike. She loved spending time with the Grumpy Badger. He was excellent company. The fact that she had to spend her entire time focusing on not jumping on him . . . *that* was a bit of a problem.

Kate gave herself a little shake. This happened every time she tried to give herself a pep-talk - she just ended up listing the reasons why she liked Mike in the first place. It really didn't help matters in the slightest!

'Come on, Kate!' she muttered.

'Yeah, come on Kate!' came a chuckle from behind her.

She whipped around to find the man himself standing, holding open the door to the cafe, laughing at her.

'Hello!' she said with a grin that she hoped might cover up the pure mortification going on underneath.

'Hello yourself! What's up? You've been standing there muttering to yourself for ages!' he laughed.

Kate straightened her shoulders. Sod it, she'd just gloss over that little comment and cut to the chase. 'I've come to warn you about Veronica!' she said.

'Uh oh. That sounds like a job to do over a coffee - fancy one?'

Kate nodded and Mike grinned at her, indicating for her to follow him into the cafe.

He made his way around the other side of the counter, clapping his barista on the shoulder. 'I've got this one, Robbie,' he grinned.

'Okay boss - just remember Kate likes a double dose of hazelnut - and don't be stingy on the froth!'

Mike snorted and raised his eyebrows at Kate. 'Do I detect a regular in our midst?!'

'What?' demanded Kate, blustering and trying to cover up her blush. 'So I like to support other Seabury businesses . . . and sometimes it's nice to grab a coffee at a different beach!' she winked at Robbie.

'Right you are,' laughed Mike.

Plus, there's more chance I'll bump into you over here!

Kate scrunched up her nose and turned away from the counter to stare around the space that used to house the town's surf shop. It had gone out of business ages ago and had been such a sad, empty space right in the heart of Seabury before Mike had come in and worked his magic on it.

It was absolutely gorgeous in here - though a small part of her really did hate to admit it! It couldn't be more different from The Sardine if it tried. Whereas her place was tiny, eclectic and filled with seaside charm, New York Froth was a bit like having coffee in a beautiful old public library. The dark wood interior was lit with the warm glow of golden wall lights and quirky pendulums.

Several walls were papered to look like they held massive bookshelves, groaning with vintage volumes, but Mike had made sure to include several real bookshelves around the space too, and had even set up a book-swap in one of the back cabinets that was proving to be incredibly popular.

Sure - Kate came in here to hang out with Mike and to grab a coffee at a different beach. But she also came in here because it was simply a lovely place to spend time away from work. There had been quite a lot of muttering around town to begin when she was spotted drinking coffee in here - but then, as Mike spent just as much time hanging out at The Sardine, it soon blew over.

Right now, there was a gaggle of young mums taking over most of the back of the cafe. Their fleet of giant buggies was parked along the wall and they had an entire table groaning with coffees, pastries and sippy cups for the gang of rampaging toddlers who were clambering all over the leather sofas with gleeful abandon.

'Right. One very frothy hazelnut latte. Anything else?' asked Mike, popping the tall mug down on the counter next to his own minuscule espresso cup.

'Don't forget her biscotti or you'll be in trouble!' chuckled Robbie, grabbing the metal tongs and placing one on her saucer for her.

'Cheers Robbie!' she grinned.

'Outside or inside?' said Mike, as she picked up her cup and he followed her with his own.

'Inside. By the window?' said Kate. As much as she loved seeing the toddlers having fun on the sofas, she could really do with Mike being able to hear what she had to say!

'So, what's up?' he asked, smiling at her as he took the chair opposite hers.

'Veronica,' sighed Kate.

'Mm-hmm?'

'It's that wedding. She just tried to wangle twenty cake boxes. She got Lou to agree to a fifty per cent discount and then paid by cheque.'

'Ah. Not great.'

Kate smiled ruefully and shook her head. 'I've just been round there to warn her not to strong-arm my staff.'

'You know, I love your protective side!' laughed Mike.

Kate felt that treacherous blush rise to her cheeks again so she grabbed her coffee and took a sip. Not bad at all! Mike Pendle knew his way around a coffee machine, that was for certain.

'So?' said Mike, 'what happened?'

'Not much. I told her I'd give her a ten per cent discount - because I'd give that to any local business. And I told her she'd need to pay in full by cash or card by the end of the week.'

'And you don't think she'll do that?'

Kate chuckled. 'Not a chance.'

'I'm sorry you lost the order, though.'

Kate shook her head. 'I'm not. She'd be a nightmare from beginning to end. I just feel sorry for Annabel.'

'Whose that?' said Mike, looking confused.

'The poor bride. I met her on my delivery round. Her and her other half seem really lovely. I hate that they're going to be so disappointed.'

'You don't know they will,' said Mike gently.

'I've just been in there. The place is a biohazard, Mike!'

He wrinkled his nose. 'That bad?'

'I'm surprised she hasn't been shut down,' she said seriously.

'But surely this couple must have looked around before booking?'

Kate shrugged. She wouldn't have put it past Veronica to get around that somehow. 'She *is* doing up the dining room though. It's looking really nice, actually, but the rest of the place is awful.'

'I feel a bit sorry for her. Sounds like she's struggling,' said Mike looking thoughtful.

'I know,' sighed Kate. 'I do too . . . only . . . I would probably feel worse if she hadn't just tried to diddle me out of a bunch of money.'

Mike snorted. 'Good point! But wait - you said you wanted to warn me?'

Kate nodded, taking another comforting sip of

coffee. 'She's going to be getting desperate. I can't believe she thought she'd manage to squeeze that little ruse past me . . .'

'She was relying on your soft side,' said Mike with a gentle smile.

'I'm afraid I don't have much of one of those anymore,' sighed Kate. 'Not after everything that's happened recently.'

Mike raised his eyebrows. 'You do. You're just a little bit more protective of it, that's all.'

Kate looked down at the table where her hand lay. Without thinking, Mike had just laid his own large paw over hers, and the feeling of his warm skin against hers was making her tingle.

Get a grip, Kate!

She forced a smile at him, and then as naturally as she could, took her hand away to pick up her mug.

'So,' said Mike, draining his own coffee as if nothing untoward had just happened, 'you think she might move on to me?'

Kate nodded. 'I wouldn't put it past her.'

'But I don't do cakes.'

'You do pastries - plus, she might try to get to Sarah through you rather than me,' she said, suddenly realising that she wouldn't put that past Veronica either.

'Would you mind if I did something for her - I mean, if she does ask?' said Mike.

'Not at all,' said Kate in surprise. 'I guess I just don't want her taking the piss out of anyone! Most of the stalwarts in town know exactly what she's like - that's why she waited until I was out on my rounds to approach Lou.'

'And that's why you think she might try to rope me in,' Mike nodded. 'I just hate the thought of that couple being let down, that's all.'

'I know what you mean,' sighed Kate. 'Just make sure you get paid upfront, that's all.'

'Got it!' said Mike. 'I'll make sure the staff know too - just in case. And thanks for the heads up!'

'Of course,' said Kate, smiling at him. 'It's what friends do, right?'

'Friends,' echoed Mike quietly, looking out of the window across at the sea. 'Right.'

'I guess I'd better-'

'Kate?' said Mike, suddenly turning back towards her and fixing his gaze on her. 'Do you think . . . I mean, would you like . . . no, never mind.'

'Mike, what?' She let out a little laugh, trying to brush off his awkwardness, but she suddenly had a strange sensation in her chest. It was like a cross between excited butterflies and impending doom.

'I just . . . I'd really like to . . .' he paused again and ran one hand through his hair making the dark strands stick wildly up in the air. Kate had the sudden urge to reach up and smooth them back into place. Instead, she firmly wrapped her hands around her almost-empty mug so that she wouldn't be tempted to do anything stupid without thinking about it.

'Man, this used to be so easy when I was a teenager,' laughed Mike. 'Kate, would you like to come out with me for a meal one evening?'

Kate smiled at him uncertainly. 'What, with you and Sarah?' she said lightly. She had a pretty good idea that this wasn't what he was asking at all, but she needed to check.

Mike shook his head. 'No, I mean just with me,' he paused and cleared his throat. 'Like - a date. I'd really like to take you out on a date.'

And there it was. The sense of doom settled in her chest. She'd dreaded this moment - not because she didn't want it to happen - but because she wanted it to happen so much and knew that she'd have to give him an answer that would totally suck for both of them.

'I'm sorry. I can't,' she said quietly.

Mike shook his head with a smile that didn't come quick enough to mask the look of hurt that crossed his face.

'It isn't that I don't want to,' she said hesitantly.

'You don't have to explain,' said Mike.

'I do. I love your company but . . . Mike, I'm just not ready.'

'Is it because of Sarah?' he asked, clearly trying to keep his voice as light as possible.

Kate let out a snort of surprise. 'Are you kidding me? She's been on my case about asking you out for weeks!'

Mike groaned and covered his face with his hands.

'Uhhhh, kiiiiids!' he whined through his fingers, making her laugh.

'It's just this whole mess with Tom,' she sighed.

'You don't think I'm like him, do you?' said Mike, looking even more horrified, if that was at all possible.

'No, of course not. But . . . until that's done and dusted, I just feel like I'm in limbo. I need a clean break from that mistake - and let's not even *mention* "Pierre",' she muttered. 'Maybe I need a bit of time to put that behind me too.'

Mike nodded. 'Okay. I mean, I get where you're coming from. I've felt the same with Sienna - not that it bothered her in the slightest - I think she moved on before we'd even officially split up!'

'God, I'm sorry!' said Kate.

'Don't be. It was over between us long before it was over if you know what I mean.'

Kate nodded. 'Yeah, sadly I do.' She heaved a sigh. Logically she knew that she'd just made the right decision, but that didn't stop her heart from wanting to kick her stupid, logical brain in the nuts for making her miss out on what she knew would have been an amazing first date.

'Kate . . .' said Mike, glancing at her. 'I know now's not the right time, but is there a chance . . . you know, maybe one day, when things are a bit more sorted? Or is this a gentle way of you telling me it's a "never" kind of no?'

Kate looked at him. Mike looked like he was forcing

himself to meet her eye, and he was definitely looking quite pink in the face by this point. She had to forcibly stop herself from leaning over and grabbing him.

She took a deep breath. It wasn't fair to lead him on, was it? It wasn't fair to make him wait around for something that might never happen.

'I . . .' she trailed off as her heart gave her head a firm punch and took over. 'It's definitely *not* a never kind of no,' she said quietly.

'So, maybe one day?' he said, his eyes twinkling.

'Maybe.'

CHAPTER 8

Kate yawned widely and dragged the two little tables out onto the pavement in front of The Sardine. It looked like it was going to be yet another beautiful crisp, autumn day. The sea was calm and the early morning mist made everything look magical. She could hear the Chilly Dippers squealing and giggling on their early-morning swim from here, and it made her smile. She hoped Stanley was behaving himself and hadn't decided on a spot of impromptu seal-watching this morning!

Kate let out a huge sigh and smiled. Ever since Mike had asked her out on that date, she'd felt lighter, somehow. Happier. Which was ridiculous, considering that she'd turned him down, but still . . . something about that moment had made her realise that there was a life full of new possibilities and adventures waiting for her beyond this mess with Tom. There were things to look forward to, even if she wasn't quite ready to open up to them yet.

She trundled back indoors and headed into the little galley kitchen. She'd prepared a vat of spiced pumpkin and squash soup the day before using some of the beauties Charlie had brought her from his allotment. It had plenty of cumin in it and was sweet and spicy and very warming - just what the Chilly Dippers would need after a cold dip in the October sea. As soon as it was hot, she'd pop it into the soup kettle and then head down for a quick wander along the beach and watch the girls in action before starting the day.

As soon as she reached the little set of stone steps that lead down onto the beach, Kate spotted the rather unusual sight of Paula, wrapped in a towel, sitting on the beach. From here, it looked like she was watching the others as they either pranced around in the shallows or swam in steady breast-stroke backwards and forwards along the stretch of beach, never venturing too far from the shore.

Kate carefully climbed down the sandy steps and made her way over towards her friend. She'd changed into her swimsuit with the others in the cafe, but Kate could see that she'd pulled a pair of jogging bottoms back onto her legs and had her vast, fluffy towel wrapped tightly around her shoulders.

What was even stranger about this sight was that Stanley was sitting next to her. Kate frowned with worry. His fur was completely dry, so he clearly hadn't been in for a swim either. Paula had her arms wrapped around the big bear, and now Kate was closer she could see that her friend's face was buried in Stanley's neck.

She walked quietly towards them, and it was only when she was about ten paces away that she noticed Paula's entire body was shuddering with wracking sobs.

Stanley glanced up at Kate with worried eyes, but he didn't stir. Clearly, he knew that Paula needed him right now, and there was no way he was going to desert her - not even to greet his best friend.

'Paula love?' said Kate quietly, sitting down next to her, but leaving a space between them. She didn't want to startle her friend, and until she knew what was going on, she didn't want to touch her in case she'd hurt herself.

Paula looked up in surprise at the sound of her voice, and Kate couldn't help but let out a gasp. Paula's eyes were red and puffy - she'd clearly been crying for a while. It broke Kate's heart to think of her here, all on her own, when the other Dippers were having fun so close by. They obviously hadn't noticed that there was something dreadfully amiss with their troublemaker-in-chief.

'Kate!' she said, taking one hand away from Stanley's coat and mopping her eyes with the edge of her towel. 'Sorry! I thought I was on my own. I didn't mean for anyone to see me like this.'

'Don't apologise!' said Kate quickly. She wanted to reach out and hug her friend but something held her back.

'Ignore me,' snuffled Paula.

'Fat chance!' muttered Kate. 'What's wrong?'

'Seriously - ignore me,' said Paula again, with a wobbly attempt at a smile. 'It's probably just insane hormones or something.'

Kate frowned. She knew when she was being fobbed off, but equally, she also knew what it was like when you just weren't quite ready to talk about something.

'Okay,' said Kate. 'But you know I'm right here - if you want to talk?'

Paula let out a huge, shuddering sigh and nodded. 'Thanks. I know. And . . . we will, just not yet - if that's okay?'

'Of course it is,' said Kate. 'Want a human hug?' she asked, smiling across at Stanley.

Paula nodded, and Kate scooted her bum closer so that she could wrap her arm around her friend. Paula snuggled into her, resting her head against Kate's shoulder, but she kept her other arm firmly wrapped around the warm, comforting fluff-mountain that was Stanley.

When Paula's breathing had calmed down and she seemed to have settled a bit, Kate felt like she could talk again. 'Didn't fancy a swim this morning?' she asked lightly.

'I just . . . I thought I did, but then I decided I just wanted to watch the others doing what they love, you know?'

'It's a good sight!' said Kate with a smile. 'I could hear them laughing from inside The Sardine!'

'Yeah. They're like family to me, this bunch.'

Kate swallowed a lump that rose suddenly to her throat. Paula sounded so sad. Completely heartbroken in fact.

'Ignore me,' said Paula again with a little laugh as a couple of fresh tears escaped. 'Like I said - probably hormones.'

'Mm,' mumbled Kate noncommittally.

'I'm really sorry Stanley hasn't had his swim, though! I tried to get him to go down to the sea with the others, but he just glued himself to my side!' She stroked his head gently and Kate saw Stanley lean his weight against her.

'He always knows when someone needs a bit of extra TLC,' said Kate, squeezing her friend's shoulders.

'He really is the best dog,' said Paula.

'He is. And you know where he is whenever you need an extra floofy hug or a bit of unconditional comfort. Stanley's right here for you.'

Paula nodded gratefully. 'Thanks Kate,' she said, staring ahead at the sea.

'I'm right here for you too,' said Kate quietly.

Paula turned to face her, and even though her lips were still quivering with whatever emotion she was currently struggling with, she gave her a grateful smile. 'Kate - whatever happens, you can always talk to me too, okay? Promise we'll always be friends?' said Paula, her chin quivering.

'Oh love,' sighed Kate, gathering her friend to her with both arms as she broke down into tears again, 'of course I promise.'

By the time the Dippers had finished steaming up the windows and filling The Sardine with the sound of laughter, Kate felt a bit like a wrung sponge. Lou had cheerfully agreed to head off and take Trixie out on her rounds, leaving Kate to man the cafe alone until it was time for Sarah's shift to start. Stanley had stayed behind too - glued to Paula's side as she picked at her breakfast and joined in with the general banter in a half-hearted way.

'Do you think anyone noticed anything?' she asked as she gave Kate a quick, final hug before heading off to work.

Kate pulled back, gave her a reassuring smile and shook her head. 'You're all good. Hope today gets better - and let's catch up soon, okay?'

Paula nodded gratefully, gave Stanley a final pat and headed off.

For the next ten minutes, every time Kate turned around Stanley was right there, staring at her in concern. The third time she nearly tripped over him as she cleared away the detritus of the Dippers' breakfasts, she gave in. Plonking the plates she was carrying back down onto the tabletop, she knelt down next to him on the floor.

'What's up, boy?' she asked gently.

Stanley wiggled his beautiful eyebrows at her, let out a pitiful whine and then coming as close as he could, he leant his heavy head on her shoulder.

'Oh, my poor bear!' she said in surprise. 'Your turn for a hug, huh?' she asked, gently wrapping her arms around him and holding him close.

They stayed like that in the empty cafe for several long minutes until Kate heard the door open and close.

'Hey - are you okay?' came Sarah's voice from overhead, full of surprise at having found her boss on the floor with her arms wrapped around Stanley.

'*I'm* fine,' said Kate, smiling up at her. 'Stanley needed a hug though, didn't you lad?' she said, pulling back at last and ruffling his ears. 'You better now?'

He wagged his tail, then stood up and turned to greet Sarah.

'Looks like you've worked your magic on him!' laughed Sarah, as he nosed the pocket of her jacket where she usually kept a stash of his favourite treats.

'I think it's just one of those days,' shrugged Kate.

'Sooo, how's project Grumpy Badger going?' said

Sarah, peeling off her jacket and throwing a cheeky wink at Kate over her shoulder as she hung it on the pegs.

'Don't start,' sighed Kate. Normally she didn't mind one bit - okay, she *did* mind - but she could deal with it. But after the ridiculously emotional start to the day, and the fact that she knew she wouldn't be able to stop worrying about what was bothering Paula until they had the chance to meet up for a proper chat, Kate just wasn't in the mood.

'Sorry,' said Sarah, looking mildly surprised.

'No,' said Kate, 'I'm sorry. I didn't mean to snap - I'm just getting it from every direction at the moment.'

'Well,' said Sarah, her voice thoughtful, 'if you don't want people talking about you guys and assuming things are . . . erm . . . progressing . . . perhaps sitting in the window of New York Froth and holding hands is a bad idea?'

'Holding hands?!' squeaked Kate. 'We weren't holding hands!'

'Calm down,' laughed Sarah, 'it isn't illegal, you know!'

'But we *weren't* . . . *oooooh* . . .' That moment when she'd told Mike she no longer had a soft side, and he'd briefly laid his hand on hers.

'Don't try to pretend it didn't happen, because I saw you with my own eyes,' smirked Sarah.

'I was . . . erm . . . upset about something, and your

dad was just trying to comfort me, that's all. Just - as a friend,' she added.

Sarah's face fell. 'But you guys would be *so* good together! And I know you like him.'

Kate bit her lip. She didn't want to snap at the girl again, this *was* her father they were talking about after all, but equally, she really *did* need to put an end to this - for her own sanity, if nothing else.

'Look,' she said carefully, 'I *do* like your dad. He's a lovely guy and I'm really enjoying having him as a friend.'

'So-!' Sarah started, her eyes shining in excitement.

Kate quickly held her hand up to stop her in her tracks. 'So - I've just told him that I'm not ready to be anything other than friends.'

'Aw, but-'

'You get it, don't you?' said Kate, looking at her appealingly. 'I had a bad experience with Pierre . . . Ian . . . whatever his name was, and don't even get me started on Tom! Until this mess with getting the divorce sorted out is all over and done with - it's just hanging over me. It's not that I'm not ready for a relationship with your dad - it's more that I'm not ready for one with *anyone*.'

Sarah chewed her lip a moment. 'Okay - I guess I *do* get it,' she sighed.

'Good,' said Kate with a small smile.

'And I'll back off a bit. Sorry - I was just having a bit of fun because I know how much he likes you.'

'That's okay - but thanks.' Kate tried her best to shut up the inner voice that was now jumping up and down like an excited six-year-old shouting *Mike lurves Ka-aaate, Mike lurves Ka-aaaate!*

'Morning ladies!'

'Hey George!' said Sarah brightly, turning to take a wodge of envelopes from their regular postie. 'We've got your cake box if you want to take it now? Or did you want to pop back in when you're done?'

'I'll swing by for a coffee this afternoon when I've finished for the day, thanks Sarah,' he smiled. 'If anyone spots me doing my rounds with my cakes, I'll end up with an empty box again - that's what happened last month - I barely got a look in!' he chuckled.

'Now there's a bit of advertising I would never have dreamed up in a million years,' said Kate. 'And for that - this afternoon's coffee is on the house.'

'Ah, you're an angel. See you both later then!' he said, raising his hand in a wave as he strolled back out onto the seafront.

'Here,' said Sarah, handing the post to Kate before heading outside to make sure their little yard was all set up to receive the first customers of the day.

Kate flicked through the pile, fully expecting to be able to bung the whole lot into the recycling. There were the usual circulars from the local garden centre and a pamphlet for double glazing. Tucked neatly in between them was a manilla envelope that made her heart plummet. She half wished that she hadn't spotted it at all, but she'd already learned the hard way that envelopes like this shouldn't be ignored.

Kate quickly checked over her shoulder and, seeing that she was alone, tore the envelope open, barely keeping the grimace off her face.

Sure enough, it was yet another letter from Tom's solicitor. Some kind of bill, by the looks of things. As she scanned the list of figures in front of her, her jaw dropped, and when she reached the total at the bottom of the second side of A4, she let out a fluent string of swearwords.

'Pretty fruity for a Wednesday morning!'

Kate spun around, only to find both Lionel and Sarah staring at her.

'So sorry Lionel . . . it's Tom again.'

'What a prat,' said Sarah, wandering past and giving Kate a comforting pat on the shoulder.

'Hand it over,' grunted Lionel.

'I . . .'

'Please, Kate. Let me help you. This has gone on for long enough, don't you think?'

She wasn't sure if it was the memory of Paula sobbing into Stanley's coat, or the massive sense of loss she'd felt when she'd turned Mike down just because she hadn't managed to clear all this mess up yet, but something in Kate finally gave way.

'Here,' she said, handing him the letter. 'He's charging me for all of his solicitor's time - which is bloody massive because he's being such a dumbass -

and all his mediation costs. On the second sheet, they've outlined the costs of going to court . . . and I just can't . . . I can't . . .' Kate paused and swallowed. She *would not* burst into tears in the middle of the cafe. Not in front of poor Sarah. Not in front of Lionel. What if a customer came in?

'Come out to the yard with me to take my order a second?' he said to her, glancing quickly over at Sarah.

Kate nodded. 'Back in a sec,' she mumbled and followed Lionel outside.

The minute they reached the empty courtyard, Kate sank into one of the pretty metal chairs and rubbed her face hard with her hands. She *had* to get her act together.

'Sorry - I thought it would be best to speak in private a moment,' said Lionel with a look of concern on his face.

Kate nodded. 'It's not fair on Sarah!'

'No. I'm sure she had enough drama when her parents went through it all.'

Kate nodded.

'Kate, please, *please* let me call in that favour with Philip. This has gone on too long, and I don't know what these fellows are playing at, but it's not cricket!'

'I guess I deserve it!' said Kate.

Lionel shook his head firmly. 'Even if you had misbehaved during your marriage, the law doesn't take it into account in the slightest unless we were talking about extreme violence or something similar. But you didn't - you simply made a mistake and married a man you didn't love.'

Kate nodded miserably, because recently she'd started to realise just how different it *did* feel when you really started to fall for someone.

'Can I pass this on to Philip?' he said, waving the letter. 'Let me help you.'

Kate held her breath for a moment, staring straight past Lionel out at the sea. She'd love nothing more than to get on with her life. It was time.

'Okay - yes. Yes please, Lionel. I would love your help. This has gone on way too long. You're right.'

'Wonderful!' said Lionel, smiling broadly. 'Just you wait, we'll have this all done and dusted before you know it!'

'Thank you.'

'Like I said before - we're family!'

CHAPTER 9

After the morning she'd had, Kate wanted nothing more than to disappear up to the safety of her flat and have a damn good skiving session in front of a film. If it hadn't been for the fact that she knew Paula was at work, she might have even tried to convince her friend to come over and try to get her to open up about whatever was bothering her.

As it was, the little cafe was super-busy all morning, keeping both her and Sarah run off their feet. An entire fleet of cyclists who were working their way along the south coast had arrived. They'd commandeered the little yard and her outdoor tables too - and there still wasn't enough room for them all to perch somewhere.

Kate suggested that perhaps some of them might prefer to make their way along to North Beach and head into New York Froth if they would prefer to sit inside, but every single one of them had stayed put. It had taken a good hour to make sure they all had their drinks and snacks and were happy.

Even the usually indefatigable Sarah was beginning to droop by the time Lou reappeared from the delivery round.

'Why don't you give Ethel a call?' said Lou to Kate as she took over from Sarah behind the coffee machine, giving the poor girl a much-needed break. 'Sarah's got to go in for lectures this afternoon, and I don't mean to be rude, but you look like you could do with a break too, boss!'

Kate paused and raised her eyebrows. Ethel had been in full jam-making flow over the past few weeks. Because they now had Lou, she hadn't been working quite so many shifts in the cafe - preferring to focus on the cake subscription boxes and sneaking off for romantic trysts with Charlie - but she always said that she was more than happy to step in whenever needed. Considering Kate felt like she'd already worked a twelve-hour day, this definitely counted as one of those occasions.

'You know what, I think I will give her a call,' sighed Kate.

'Good. We've all got to look after each other, right?'

Kate nodded. 'Right. And thank you for doing the rounds this morning - I really appreciate that.'

'Happy to do it whenever you need me - I love getting out and meeting everyone!'

'You might not be *quite* so keen when the rain is coming at you sideways,' laughed Kate.

'I'll leave those days to you!' chuckled Lou.

'Any issues at all today?'

'Nope!' said Lou. 'Graphika asked if I could add a couple more cake boxes to their order on Monday because they've got a bunch of interviews lined up - so that'll keep Ethel out of trouble,' she laughed, 'oh, and there was a note on the door of that holiday cottage - you know, the one where the couple for the wedding are staying?'

'Oh?' said Kate.

'Yeah - just asking if we could bring their order back here and they'll pick it up later because they're in town for a last-minute meeting with Veronica. It was very apologetic.'

'Oh, okay,' said Kate, 'well, that's no problem! What are their names again . . . Annabel and . . .? I keep forgetting the groom!'

Lou fiddled in her back pocket, drew out a crumpled note and unfolded it. 'Annabel and Lee,' she said. 'Anyway, I've already popped their order over there ready for them to collect later.'

'Fab. Right, I'll just give Ethel a quick call to see if she can cover me. Even an hour might help!'

Kate grabbed her mobile and within minutes, Ethel had cheerfully agreed to cover a couple of hours so that Kate could take a break. 'Sorry I can't do more than that, but Charlie's taking me to the pictures this afternoon,' she said, and Kate could hear the grin in her voice.

'Oh Ethel, then don't worry about it!' said Kate quickly. 'You'll want to be getting ready for your date, not working!'

'Nonsense!' laughed Ethel. 'I'll just ask Charlie to pick me up from The Sardine.'

Kate did her best to backtrack, but Ethel was having none of it and promised to be there within twenty minutes.

She was just stashing her mobile away again with a mixture of relief at being able to escape the cafe for a couple of hours and guilt for making Ethel change her plans, when Mike appeared in the doorway.

'Well, this is a nice surprise!' she said, unable to keep the smile off her face.

Mike smiled at her, but she couldn't miss the fact that he looked like his morning had been just as bad as hers.

'I've not missed Sarah, have I?' he asked, a worried note in his voice.

'No, she just nipped out the back,' said Lou. 'Would you like a coffee?'

Mike shook his head. 'No - thanks though - I've been pretty much mainlining it all morning!'

'Is everything alright?' said Kate.

'Erm, well . . . yes, but I've had a bit of sad news. My old aunt passed away suddenly last night.'

'Oh Mike, I'm so sorry,' said Kate.

'Thanks,' he said awkwardly. 'I just felt like I should tell Sarah as soon as possible. I know she's meant to have college this afternoon, but she adored Aunty Sally and they were quite close. She was more like her grandmother than an aunt.' He let out a weary sigh and rubbed his face. 'Sorry. I know I probably shouldn't have just turned up when she's still got to finish her shift.'

'Don't apologise,' said Kate gently, moving over to him and giving him an awkward pat on the arm. What she really wanted to do was throw her arms around him and give him a damn good cuddle, but she had a sneaking suspicion that wouldn't be fair.

'Hey dad!' said Sarah with a grin, appearing in the doorway and looking between Mike and Kate, an excited gleam in her eye, 'what's up?'

'I've got a bit of bad news, love,' he said. 'Grab your coat and we'll go for a wander on the beach and over to Nana's for an ice cream.'

Sarah looked at him, and Kate's heart squeezed as she saw the fear cross the young girl's face.

'Is it mum?' she said, her voice trembling, all traces of her smile now completely gone.

Mike's eyebrows shot up in surprise and he quickly shook his head. 'No love, it's not your mum. It's about Aunty Sally.'

Kate grabbed Sarah's coat and bag for her and handed them over to Mike, and both she and Lou watched them leave, Sarah grabbing her dad's hand as they pushed their way out through the door, looking more like a scared little six-year-old rather than the confident sixteen-year-old she was.

'Poor kid,' sighed Lou.

'I know,' said Kate sadly. 'Poor Mike, too. Man, can this day get any worse?'

'Don't!' squeaked Lou. 'You'll jinx it!'

They'd barely had time to turn their back on the door when Ethel bowled in.

'Ah, my hero!' said Kate, smiling at her old friend. 'Thank you so much!' she said.

'Not a problem, deary,' said Ethel quickly, looking slightly distracted.

'Sure?'

'Absolutely - but I'm afraid we might have a bit of an emergency on our hands before you head off.'

'I *told* you that you'd jinx it!' muttered Lou, making Ethel a coffee without bothering to ask if she wanted one.

'If that's my latte,' said Ethel, shooting a grateful smile at Lou, 'you'd better make a triple espresso and a cappuccino with plenty of chocolate while you're at it.'

'Who for?' said Kate.

'Come with me,' said Ethel, nodding at the door. 'I'll pop back in for the coffees in a sec, Lou love!'

Lou gave Ethel a quick thumbs up and loaded up the puck to set the Italian Stallion to work.

Ethel grabbed a pile of napkins on her way out, making Kate raise her eyebrows in question, but her friend just sighed and led her around into the little yard.

'Annabel!' said Kate, spotting the young bride-to-be perched at one of the tables in the corner. She'd been focusing on her phone screen, but as soon as she heard her name, she looked around.

Kate gasped. 'What's the matter!'

Annabel's eyes were red and puffy, and there were still tear tracks on her face. The young man opposite her stood up and held his hand out to Kate.

'Hi - you must be Kate.'

'Lee?' said Kate, assuming that this must be the groom-to-be.

'Yep, that's me.'

'It's lovely to meet you, but what's up?'

'Sorry, Kate,' sighed Annabel. 'I'm being a drama queen, that's all!'

'You are not,' said Ethel stoutly, passing her the napkins. 'She's been Veronica-d,' she added, turning to Kate.

'May I?' said Kate, pointing to the empty chair. Lee nodded, and she sank down into it.

'Veronica-d?' he muttered, as Ethel disappeared back towards the cafe.

'I'm afraid she doesn't have the best . . . erm . . . *reputation*. At least, not when it comes to customer service.'

'Oh nooooo,' said Annabel, dropping her face into her hands.

'It'll be fine, Bel!' said Lee, covering her hand with his. 'It's only the cake. I'm sure we can sort it out!'

He widened his eyes pleadingly at Kate.

'Tell me exactly what's going on,' she said. 'Only if you want to, of course!' she added, with a small smile.

'Veronica said that the person supplying the cupcakes that were meant to make up our wedding cake have let her down, and they're refusing to give our money back,' said Annabel, frowning.

Kate did her best to hold back a growl. So *that's* what the cake boxes were for? How much should she tell these two? She didn't want to talk out of turn about Veronica - not when these two still had to deal with her . . . but this was business. She wasn't sure what Veronica was up to, but it didn't exactly sound like she was being upfront with them.

She was about to ask for more details when Ethel appeared carrying a tray with three coffees as well as their order that had been due for delivery up to their cottage earlier.

'Here - coffees - and I thought maybe your lunch might make things look a bit brighter!'

'Thanks so much,' said Lee, beaming at her. 'And for bringing us straight over here.'

'Well, it was clear by the looks on your faces that you'd just had a run-in with the wicked witch of Pebble Street,' said Ethel, rolling her eyes.

Kate eyeballed her, not wanting to make the pair any more upset than they already were.

'What do you mean?' said Annabel. 'Is she really that bad? I mean, she's always been pretty . . . curt . . . when I've spoken to her, but she's always been adamant that she'd find exactly what we wanted for the big day!'

'Have you . . .' Kate paused. Ah well, they were well and truly spooked by this point anyway, so she may as well just dive in head-first. 'Have you had a proper look around The Pebble Street Hotel yet?' she asked curiously.

Annabel rolled her eyes. 'No, not yet.'

'You booked without seeing it?' said Ethel in surprise, still hovering, clearly intrigued.

'Bel's grandparents got married there,' said Lee. 'We've seen all the beautiful photos. Her grandma, Rose, passed away last year and we thought . . .' he paused and took Annabel's hand across the table. 'We thought we'd like to honour her memory.'

Kate's eyebrows shot up. *That* explained a lot.

'Veronica's having a lot of work done on the place - returning it to its former glory - so it's not safe for us to go in for a look around just yet,' said Annabel.

'We got to have a quick peek into the dining room just now through the double glass doors around the back, and it looks like it's going to be lovely,' said Lee, though Kate noticed that he looked a little bit sceptical.

'And the wedding's in-?'

'Ten days,' said Lee.

'That's why we decided to stay down here,' said

Annabel. 'So that we can be on hand as soon as we can get in to see it.'

'Erm . . .' Kate looked up at Ethel in alarm. Should she tell them that she'd been in there just a few days ago, and the place was an abomination and the only work taking place was in the dining room itself?

'Did you explain about the cake?' said Ethel, clearly trying to steer the conversation back to a slightly more manageable problem to begin with.

Annabel nodded. 'Yes.'

'Well, what I'm sure Kate's been too polite to tell you is that Veronica tried to order twenty of our cake subscription boxes for your wedding the other day.'

'Oh!' said Annabel in surprise. 'You're the company? But then . . .'

'It wasn't us that let you down,' sighed Kate. 'Like I said, Veronica has a bit of a reputation . . .'

'What do you mean?' said Lee, frowning.

'She never pays her bills,' said Ethel bluntly. 'So we can't take cheques from her anymore.'

'But she said you'd refused the order and then refused to give her the money back?' said Annabel looking confused.

Kate shook her head and sighed. 'On the contrary. I would be very happy to do the order - *if* that's what you want, though I'm sure you had something a bit more special in mind for your wedding cake than several takeaway boxes emptied out onto a stand?!'

Annabel nodded then covered her mouth with a

gasp. 'Sorry - I didn't mean that in a bad way. You know we're huge fans of yours - but I *did* expect something a bit fancier for three hundred quid!'

Ethel let out a snort. 'That thieving witch!'

'Yes, *thank* you Ethel!' said Kate quickly.

'Sorry. I . . . um, I think I'd better go and help Lou before I say something I shouldn't!'

Kate watched her bustle away, and she could tell from the set of her shoulders that her old friend was decidedly angry.

'Sorry,' said Kate, turning back to the couple, who were looking uncomfortable. 'Ethel's so straight down the line, she hates seeing Veronica pull this stuff. Look, just so you know, I haven't taken any of your money from Veronica - so you're absolutely free to go ahead and find the cake of your dreams and get her to put the order in for you.'

'But why would she say that you've got the money?' said Lee, looking baffled.

'I have no idea,' said Kate. 'Maybe she's just confused. I can assure you, I tore up the cheque in front of her and gave it back to her.'

'I just don't understand why she didn't just give you the cash,' said Annabel, shaking her head. 'Even if it wasn't what we had discussed for our cake, at least it would have been something!'

'Can I ask a personal question?' said Kate carefully.

Annabel nodded.

'Have you also paid Veronica a deposit for the hotel?'

'No,' said Lee. 'It's so important to us that we get to celebrate at The Pebble Street Hotel - and we wanted to be sure that we'd get the whole place. Veronica wasn't happy to close to other guests for the weekend unless we paid the whole fee up front, so we went ahead and did that. She's had the entire booking fee, plus the balance for catering, alcohol and the cake too.'

'And the band,' said Annabel excitedly. 'Don't forget the band!'

Kate could hear alarm bells ringing so loudly it was as though they'd been attached directly to her ears. She did her best to keep her face looking calm. She didn't want the couple to start freaking out as much as she was right now.

'If you want my advice . . .?' she paused and glanced at them, checking. Both Lee and Annabel nodded. 'Okay, I think it might be a good plan to insist that you have a look around the hotel - don't leave it any longer and don't let her weasel out of it. There isn't any work that should stop you going in.'

Lee raised his eyebrows and nodded. 'Yeah, we were just saying that to Ethel on the way over.'

'Then I'd say trust your instincts on that one. Plus - some friendly advice from someone who's had issues dealing with Veronica before - I'd ask to see all the paperwork to prove that your catering and drinks orders are sorted. It might not be a bad idea for you to make a couple of backup phone calls directly to the companies too - just to be absolutely sure it's all in hand.'

'You don't think . . .?' said Lee, looking alarmed now.

Kate tried to give him a reassuring smile, but she was pretty sure she looked just as spooked as they did by this point. 'I'm sure it'll all work out just fine - but it would put your minds at rest, wouldn't it?'

'It's a good idea, actually. Thanks Kate,' said Annabel. 'And we'll talk about the cake while we're at it too - it's getting pretty last minute to find someone now though . . .'

'Well,' said Kate, thinking on her feet, 'if you *do* get stuck, you know where I am. I'll do my best to help in any way I can - I might have a young, talented baker who'd love to work with you.'

CHAPTER 10

'Hey Sarah, how're you doing?'

Kate smiled as she watched Sarah fight to get herself and her umbrella through the door of The Sardine without drenching everything - without much luck. It was one of those days where the rain was lashing horizontally across the seafront. Somehow, she doubted they'd be particularly busy today.

Kate hadn't seen Sarah since Mike had picked her up from her shift a couple of days ago, and as she watched her shake out her long hair and bend down to cuddle Stanley, she couldn't help but notice how pale she was.

'I'm okay,' said Sarah.

Kate waited for her to say more, but she was too focused on fussing with Stanley. That was okay - she'd primed both Lou and Ethel to be a bit gentle with her over the next few days as she came to terms with the sad news about her great aunt.

Mike had texted Kate the previous day to apologise again for turning up at The Sardine and stealing Sarah away a bit early from her shift. He'd also warned her that Sarah seemed to be struggling more than he'd expected with the news.

'How're things at college?' asked Kate, trying to draw her out a bit.

Sarah shrugged. 'Pretty good. All the boring hygiene stuff is done for this term now, so we get to bake more.'

'What are you working on at the moment?' asked Kate, wanting to keep her chatting now that she'd got her going.

'Celebration cakes. That's the next bit. I could really do with a bit more practise. All my experience has been baking practical stuff. You know what I mean?'

'Yep!' said Kate. 'Good food that people want to eat. You're not going to have any problem!' she added cheerfully. 'Lots of people know how to make it look nice but forget to make the cake underneath actually taste of something!'

Sarah nodded and sighed. 'Idiots.'

Kate sniggered. 'Pretty much. But you're coming at it the right way round!'

'But I don't know any of those fancy decorating techniques!' said Sarah frowning. 'Maybe this course isn't going to teach me what I need after all . . . maybe I *should* be looking for something different . . .'

'Erm . . . I'm pretty sure they don't expect you to know everything before they've actually taught it to you,' said Kate, raising an eyebrow. It was the first time she'd heard Sarah say anything remotely negative about her course, and she was surprised. It almost sounded like she was repeating something someone else had said to her.

Sarah just shrugged at her, looking fed up.

'Anyway, don't worry,' said Kate, giving her an encouraging smile, 'if you want to give yourself a head start you could ask Lou to show you some stuff. I know she hasn't done loads of baking for us yet, but I know she's meant to be a dab hand at sugar work. And Ethel's a genius with a piping bag!'

Sarah nodded. 'Thanks Kate.' She let out a huge sigh.

'Sarah, if you ever need to talk - about anything - I'm right here, okay?'

Sarah looked at her with a frown, and for a second Kate wondered if she'd just said entirely the wrong thing. But then Sarah gave her a slightly wobbly smile. 'Thanks.'

'I hope you've got that coffee machine fired up!' boomed Lionel, bounding through the door with a grim expression on his face, water dripping off the edge of his trilby. He yanked it off of his head, gave it a quick shake and hung it from the coat stand near the door. 'It's raining cats and dogs out there!'

'Blimey, you're early!' said Kate.

'I thought you'd still be out on your rounds,' he said. 'I was expecting to have to camp out here until you got back!'

Kate grinned. 'Lou to the rescue. She really fancied the exercise, apparently - little weirdo that she is - and Stanley would have hated it out there this morning!'

'It'll be more like swimming than cycling for her out there today. I hope she's got a change of clothes for when she gets back, she's going to need it!' said Lionel.

'I'll send her up to the flat for a shower. She can borrow some of my clothes and make use of the hairdryer,' said Kate with a smile. 'I owe her that at least for letting me off the hook.'

'Did you want your usual, Lionel?' asked Sarah.

He shook his head. 'Any chance of some scrambled eggs, bacon, a couple of pieces of toast . . .'

'I can do the full works if you'd like?' said Kate trying not to show just how surprised she was.

'You know what, yes please! But can I start with a coffee? I'm gasping!'

'What's going on - Veronica on strike, or has she just not bothered to go to the cash and carry?'

'Neither. I've not seen her since yesterday!' said Lionel.

Kate paused to stare at him. 'What do you mean?'

'I reckon she's done a bunk.'

Kate shook her head. 'No chance. She'd never just disappear without telling anyone. If she was off on holiday she'd have been bragging about it for at least a couple of months by now. Blimey, I've not known her to go away even for a weekend in all the years I've known her,' said Kate. 'She's too tight for that!'

'I know, that's what I thought,' said Lionel. 'Luckily, there aren't any guests in at the moment, and there won't be until after the wedding, otherwise they'd have to fend for themselves.'

'What if she's hurt or something,' said Sarah, quietly. 'Someone should check!'

Kate glanced at Sarah and frowned. 'That's a good point.'

'She's not hurt or ill,' said Lionel. 'Same thing crossed my mind, Sarah. I've already been up to her rooms to make sure. The door was locked and this was pinned to it.'

He drew a piece of paper from his jacket pocket and handed it to Sarah as she made her way over with Lionel's coffee.

'What's it say?' asked Kate, cracking eggs as she went.

"Gone away for a while. Sort out wedding. Veronica."

'Noooo!' gasped Kate.

'What does she mean by "sort out wedding"?' said Sarah, her eyes wide.

'Lionel, I think you're right,' said Kate. 'I think she's done a runner!'

'She wouldn't . . .' said Sarah.

'Looks like she already did,' said Lionel.

'But . . . the wedding!' said Sarah.

'I'm sure we'll be able to reach her somehow and find out exactly what's going on,' said Kate, doing her best to keep her voice calm. What on earth was going *on* this week? Everything seemed to be going haywire.

'You're right,' said Lionel, nodding. 'I knew you'd be the right person to talk to.'

'Question is, what should we do first?' said Kate.

'Why don't you call dad?' said Sarah. 'He told me last night that he'd just quoted for a wedding reception. Maybe he can help?'

'He *what*?' said Kate in surprise.

Sarah nodded. 'Yeah - he said someone was looking for alternative quotes and that he was going to put some stuff together and send it through to them . . . maybe he can help you with this couple too?'

Kate blinked as a lump of hurt hit her in the chest. She couldn't exactly say anything in front of Sarah, but she couldn't believe Mike hadn't even mentioned to her that weddings were a part of his plan too.

'Okay,' she said at last, trying to keep her voice even. 'I'll go over and speak to him as soon as Lou's back and dried off. Lionel, do you mind holding off on contacting Lee and Annabel until I've had the chance to report back?'

'Of course!' he said, sipping his coffee. 'I don't have any details for them anyway. I don't know where they're staying and I've never even met the poor blighters. In actual fact, I'm not exactly sure what Veronica means by "sort out wedding" anyway.'

'You don't think she expects you to run it rather than cancel it, do you?' said Sarah thoughtfully.

Lionel's already worried expression took on a hunted air.

'Okay, wow. Halt. Let's not panic!' said Kate, plating up Lionel's breakfast and bringing it over to him. 'Let me talk to Mike first. At least maybe that'll give us some kind of alternative to offer them when we break the news. In the meantime - do you reckon you could try to find out where Veronica's disappeared to? We really could do with a bit more information on what's going on before we can do anything to help.'

Lionel stared dazedly down at his plate full of food then looked back up at Kate. 'Let me work my way through this and another coffee or two, then I'll go back over to the hotel and rummage through that eyesore she calls a desk. Maybe there'll be something on there that might give us a clue or two.'

Kate found it incredibly difficult to wait patiently for Lou to get back from the delivery round. She wanted to march straight round to New York Froth and demand an explanation from Mike about his sudden interest in catering for weddings, and why he'd not seen fit to fill her in. On the other hand, she also wanted to beg for his help to sort the whole mess out.

With Veronica AWOL, they would soon have a rightly grumpy pair of soon-to-be-weds on their hands, and a disaster like this wasn't just a problem for Veronica - it would impact the whole town if the word got out.

When Lou finally turned up - drenched to the skin and freezing cold - Kate sent her straight upstairs for a hot shower and change of clothes. She told her to take her time and make sure to get her hair properly dry too - the last thing she needed was a member of staff down with the flu!

By the time Lou emerged looking more human than drowned rat, Kate was still desperate to see Mike but she was actually grateful for the delay as it had given her enough time to calm down a bit.

'So - you two okay to man the fort while I try to sort this mess out?' she asked.

'You go, boss!' said Lou. 'But make sure you put your hood up!'

'You want to come, boy?' said Kate, looking at Stanley as she pulled on the heavy yellow mac she kept in the cafe for days like this.

Stanley stared at her from his bed under the radiator, barely bothering to lift an eyebrow in response, let alone his head.

'Okay, I'll take the hint!' laughed Kate. 'Be good, you three!'

Despite her best efforts to keep her hood up as she made the dash over to North Beach, Kate was soaked by the time she pushed her way into New York Froth. She paused on the doormat and grabbed her soggy plait, doing her best to wring out as much water as possible so that she didn't drip all the way over to the counter.

'Hi Kate!' said Robbie, grinning at her. 'Out for a swim? Not your usual morning for a visit, is it?'

'Hey,' said Kate, smiling at the lad. 'Is Mike around?'

'He is - but it's so quiet he's disappeared back upstairs to get some paperwork done.'

Kate nodded. 'Mind if I go up?'

'Be my guest,' said Robbie. 'Want me to call ahead for you?'

Kate shook her head. 'Nah. I don't want to give him the opportunity to pretend to be busy,' she laughed. 'I'm afraid it's a bit urgent.'

'Uh oh,' he said. 'That sounds ominous - you go on up!'

Kate dashed around the counter and through the swing door that led to the internal staircase. Taking two steps at a time, she quickly wound her way up to Mike's flat.

She knew it was silly, but by the time she reached the door, she was feeling ridiculously nervous. She'd only been up here once before, and that had been to help Sarah with a bunch of cake boxes she'd borrowed for a project at college.

Kate paused and did her best to smooth down her hair. She knew it would already be busy springing into ridiculous corkscrews after getting so wet. She quickly gave it up for a bad job and knocked lightly on the door.

'Kate?!'

She jumped as Mike's face appeared just a second later.

'Hi! Sorry to interrupt but we've got ourselves a bit of a situation,' she said, not really knowing quite where to start.

'Is Sarah okay?' he demanded, looking freaked.

'It's not Sarah!' she said quickly. 'Sorry, I didn't mean to scare you.'

'Oh, thank God!' he said, then looked her up and down, taking in her damp clothes. 'Come on in and warm up.' Mike, stepped back inside and indicated for her to follow him. 'So Sarah's okay?' he checked again as he lead her straight into the beautiful open-plan space.

Kate nodded. 'She's okay - a bit quiet, but I guess that's to be expected, given the circumstances,' she said, looking around the flat. It was absolutely massive. Taking up most of the front of the building, it benefitted from floor to ceiling windows that stretched across the room and looked right out over the sea. It was a spectacular sight, even on a stormy day like today.

Mike let out a sigh and ran his fingers distractedly

through his hair. 'Sarah was already upset enough about losing Aunty Sally, but we've just discovered that she's left us both money. Sarah's really struggling with that - it's like she feels guilty about it or something . . . I don't know.' He shrugged. 'Has she talked to you about it at all?'

Kate grimaced at him and shook her head. 'No. But I did tell her earlier that she can talk to me any time if she needs to.'

'Thanks Kate,' said Mike with a grateful smile. 'Don't tell her I told you about the inheritance if you don't mind? At least, not unless she brings it up first,' he said, suddenly looking awkward.

'Of course I won't,' said Kate.

'Thanks. Anyway - have a seat!'

Kate peeled off her mac, not wanting to leave a damp patch on Mike's pristine sofa. He dashed forward to take it from her and strode across the room to hang it over the back of one of the chairs in the kitchen area.

'You know, I'd forgotten what a beautiful job your guys did on this place!' said Kate, distracted for a moment by just how lovely it was in here. It was painted a very dark green - but with the light pouring through the windows, it felt calming rather than dark - in spite of the gloomy day outside.

'Thanks!' said Mike, coming back over towards her. 'We love it. Anyway, what's up?'

'Well,' said Kate, perching on the sofa as Mike sank

down onto the other end, staring at her intently, 'we need to talk weddings.'

Mike let out a spluttering cough. 'Bit early for all that, isn't it?' he laughed.

Kate raised her eyebrows. Perhaps he was just as nervous about her being here as she was. Something warm bloomed in her chest and she felt her earlier irritation with him soften a bit.

'Look,' she said, giving him a smile, 'there's a bit of a problem at The Pebble Street Hotel.'

CHAPTER 11

'So, we have no idea where she's gone, why she's gone or when she's coming back,' said Kate. She'd just spent the last five minutes filling Mike in on everything that she knew so far. 'Anyway, someone's got to talk to Lee and Annabel and tell them what's happened - and Sarah suggested I talk to you first.'

'Why?' said Mike looking worried.

'Because she said . . .' Kate swallowed down her urge to start getting cross with him for not telling her about his plans. 'She said you've just been asked to quote for a wedding reception, so you might be able to help with an alternative for these two as well.'

'Well,' said Mike, 'this isn't quite how I wanted to tell you about all this.'

'All what?' said Kate.

'The wedding I was approached about. It's actually for the same couple you're talking about.'

'Okay - now I'm completely confused,' said Kate.

'You suggested that they chase up their bookings with Veronica, didn't you - and insist on seeing the hotel?' he asked.

Kate nodded.

'Well - they did both those things. Veronica still wouldn't let them in to look around the hotel - said it would be too dangerous - but they made the phone calls. The caterers were booked but hadn't received their payments. The wine supplier had no record of any order, and the band had already cancelled the date because they hadn't received any money either.'

Kate's hand flew to her mouth, her eyes wide. No cake, no band, no food, no drink.

'What did they do?' she breathed.

'Asked for their money back so that they could find alternatives,' said Mike, 'and then approached me to ask for a quote for catering as well as any suggestions I might have for the rest of it.'

'Oh,' said Kate, her spine stiffening. 'I had no idea you were planning on taking New York Froth in that direction!'

'Kate,' he sighed, 'I didn't. I don't. But these guys are desperate, and I thought . . . I thought that maybe between us, we could do something for them. You were just telling me the other day that you'd like to do that with Trixie . . .'

'I did,' said Kate in surprise, 'but *one day* - in the future. We don't have a venue or enough staff, or . . . well . . . anything!'

'I didn't promise them anything - I just thought I could put some ideas together and run them past you to see what you thought. Then, if we thought we could make it work, we could give them a quote and see whether they wanted to go for it.'

'You wanted us to work together?' said Kate, double-checking she'd understood him properly.

Mike nodded, looking hopeful and excited.

'But we're not *ready*, Mike!' she said, trying her best to stomp on her exasperation. 'They're getting married in less than two weeks!'

'I know,' said Mike, 'but I just really wanted to help!'

'In case you hadn't noticed,' said Kate in a low voice, 'I managed to run my business perfectly well before you arrived in town. I don't need your help!'

'I didn't mean you,' said Mike with a frown. 'As of yesterday Lee and Annabel no longer have the reception of their dreams lined up. It's *them* I wanted to help. And . . . and I thought it would be an adventure for us to work on this together. I thought it would be fun!' He let out a huge sigh. 'Clearly I'm an idiot,' he added as an afterthought.

'You're not an idiot,' muttered Kate, standing up and going over to stare out at the sea, trying to make some kind of sense of the jumble of thoughts that were whizzing around her head. 'Look, let's forget this whole joint-catering thing for just a second while I try to get this straight. Lee and Annabel cancelled their booking at the hotel and got their money back from Veronica?'

'Yes and no,' said Mike. 'They cancelled the booking. Veronica tried to give them a cheque for what she owed them - but after the dire warnings you and Ethel had given them, they knew better than to accept it.'

'Thank goodness for small mercies!' said Kate, turning back to look at Mike. 'But they *did* get their money back?'

'Nope,' said Mike with a heavy sigh. 'Veronica told them she'd need to visit her bank to arrange it for them today.'

'And now she's gone,' said Kate, a sick feeling hitting her in the stomach.

'Now she's gone,' echoed Mike. 'Somehow, I can't imagine Veronica popped into the bank before pulling her disappearing act.'

'Well . . . shit,' sighed Kate.

'Pretty much,' nodded Mike.

'What are we going to do?' said Kate.

'Well,' said Mike, 'for starters, someone's going to have to tell Annabel and Lee.'

Kate nodded. 'Lionel's back at the hotel trying to see if he can find any information on where Veronica's gone. Maybe we should go and find out if he's got anywhere with that - then we can all come up with a plan?'

'Sure,' said Mike with a shrug. There was a slightly mutinous expression on his face. 'But only if you're sure you *want my help?*'

Kate flinched. She *knew* she shouldn't have thrown that at him. It hadn't been fair. 'I'm really sorry,' she said. 'I didn't mean that.'

'Yes, you did,' sighed Mike, 'but it's fine, I get it. I know The Sardine is your baby and I've got so much respect for what you've achieved. I would *never* presume to know better - because I really, *really* don't. It's just . . . I just really like spending time with you, and I thought . . . never mind.'

'What?' said Kate softly, sinking back down on the sofa, not taking her eyes off of him. 'What did you think?'

'I thought it would be fun to make someone's big day special together - and that maybe it would remind us both that not all marriages end up like our two disasters!'

Kate snorted out a laugh. It had been the last thing she'd been expecting him to say - but it was just about perfect.

'Come on,' she chuckled, grabbing his hand and hauling him to his feet. 'Let's go and try to save this shit-show!'

'Should we just go in or knock?' said Mike, awkwardly pushing his damp hair back and staring at the peeling paint of the door to The Pebble Street Hotel.

'Both?' said Kate.

'Good call,' laughed Mike. He knocked loudly then turned the handle and cracked the door open. 'Hel-looooo?' he called.

'Come on in!' came Lionel's voice.

Kate followed Mike into the foyer, only to spot the top of Lionel's head behind the reception desk. He was on his hands and knees rifling through the old desk drawers. There were piles of paper strewn all over the foyer floor.

'Try not to step on the paperwork,' he laughed, peeping over at them. 'As I was going through it, I figured I may as well try to set it in some kind of order. Veronica's going to kill me for doing this anyway - if she ever finds out - so I thought if I tidy up a bit for her she might go a bit easier on me!'

'I really wouldn't worry about Veronica right now,' sighed Kate, staring around at the heaps of paperwork. 'Did you manage to find anything useful in all this?'

Lionel grabbed the edge of the desk and hauled himself to his feet with a groan before dropping into the desk chair. 'Useful - not really. Surprising - definitely!'

Kate frowned. That sounded ominous. 'Do you want to go back over to The Sardine to talk about it?' she said, wrinkling her nose against the cabbage-y smell that still seemed to be lingering in the old building.

'I would say yes, but . . . well, I think it's probably better that we talk about this in private first.'

Kate nodded. 'I guess you're right. Plus, we need to fill you in too - Mike knows more about what's happened with Veronica and the wedding.'

'What *is* that smell,' said Mike distractedly, wrinkling his nose and looking around, clearly taking in just how filthy the place was.

'Sadly,' said Lionel, getting to his feet and gathering a small pile of papers off the desktop, 'that's the kitchen. Why do you think I haven't eaten anything here for months?'

Kate pulled a face. 'It's making me feel a bit sick.'

'Tell me about it,' said Lionel. 'Look, let's go up to my place to talk, shall we?'

'Only if you're sure,' said Mike. 'Or we can go over to mine if you'd prefer?'

'I'm not going back out into that weather unless I have to!' said Lionel. 'Come on, let's go up and I'll put the kettle on!'

They followed him up two flights of stairs and then along the hallway of the third floor. Things weren't any better up here. It looked like these rooms hadn't been used in ages. The bedroom doors stood open, and as they walked past Kate noticed that most of the beds were unmade and the rooms clearly hadn't been cleaned in aeons. The dust lay thick on every surface and even the carpet seemed to have a grey-brown extra layer of the stuff.

'Doesn't Veronica ever come up here?' she asked in surprise.

'I don't think she bothers,' said Lionel. 'She sacked Annie the last cleaner months ago - she dared to ask for her pay on time!'

'Sounds about right,' muttered Mike.

'Yes, well,' said Lionel. 'I'm afraid I've tried to keep out of it as much as possible.'

'It must be so sad for you, having to pass all this on your way in and out all the time,' said Kate, drawing a finger along the edge of a bookshelf and then flicking the thick ball of dust she'd gathered onto the floor.

'Actually, I don't tend to come this way anymore. Like you said - it's depressing! I've been using the fire escape steps to come and go, and basically pretending that my apartment has nothing to do with the rest of the place! Today's the first time I've been down this way in ages, and only because I ran out of coffee!' He paused and let out a long sigh. 'It makes me really sad, you know. It used to be a joy living here. I loved popping down to the bar of an evening for a nightcap, meeting the guests and then sharing breakfast with them the following morning. But it's never been the same since Veronica took over.'

'I'm surprised you've stayed as long as you have!' said Mike.

Lionel shrugged. 'I love my home. But you're right.

Maybe it's time to move on. Anyway - looks like I might not have much of a choice in the matter very soon,' he said, tapping the pile of paperwork he was carrying.

Kate's heart squeezed at the sorrow in his voice. She was about to ask him what he meant when they came to a halt in front of a dark wooden double door.

'Here we are!' said Lionel, taking a large key from his pocket. He fitted the key into the old fashioned lock and then beckoned for them to follow him in.

'Wow!' said Mike, wandering into the sitting room and staring around him. 'I thought my place had a good view, but this is . . . amazing!'

Lionel smiled at him over his shoulder as he flicked on a large standard lamp which came to life with a golden glow. 'Now you can see why I fought so hard to stay!'

'Uh - *yes!'* said Kate.

Lionel's suite clearly took up a good portion of this floor, and the sitting room was situated right on the corner of the building. It had huge windows set in both the outside walls - one looking out over towards West Beach and the other looking out over towards North Beach. The place was filled with sea, and clouds, and glimpses of Seabury.

'I've lived here for years but I never get tired of this view,' he sighed. 'Now then, why don't you both grab a seat and I'll pop the kettle on.'

Kate followed Mike over to a petrol-blue, buttoned

leather sofa and sank down into its worn embrace. She was desperately trying not to be nosy, but she couldn't keep her eyes from darting around, taking in the details of Lionel's sanctuary. It was a cosy, comfortable gentleman-cave. The inner walls were completely lined floor-to-ceiling with bookshelves that were groaning with what looked to be everything from huge art reference books to small, gold embossed, soft leather classics. Kate longed to get up and have a proper look through them, but she kept her bum firmly in her seat.

'What a beautiful place,' said Mike as their eyes met.

'I know,' said Kate in a low voice. 'It's like we've walked into a different era!'

'Or into an entirely different building at the very least!' laughed Mike.

'Here we go,' said Lionel, reappearing and popping a delicate silver tea tray down onto the table in front of the sofa.

Kate smiled at the three beautiful bone-china cups sitting in their saucers alongside the old brown and white striped teapot.

'What a treat,' she sighed, 'thanks Lionel.'

'My pleasure,' he said, picking up the metal strainer and pouring for them all. 'Help yourself to milk and sugar,' he said, settling himself into the armchair across from them. 'Now then - tell me what you've discovered about the wedding!'

Mike glanced at Kate and she nodded encouragingly. 'Go on,' she said, taking a sip of her tea, 'you do the honours!'

By the time Mike had filled Lionel in, the old man's eyebrows had practically disappeared into his mop of silver hair.

'Well, well, well,' he said, puffing out a breath. 'I knew old Veronica was a pain in the derrière, but I hadn't thought she'd be capable of this,' he sighed. 'And now she's done a runner with Lee and Annabel's money.'

'I know!' said Kate, shaking her head. 'But - you said you'd found something in all those papers?' she said, pointing at the little pile Lionel had left, face-down on the table.

He nodded. 'Well, for a start . . . it looks like she's gone to Australia!'

'*What?!*' squeaked Mike, choking on a sip of tea.

Lionel shrugged. 'I found booking details for her flight.'

'But why Australia?' said Kate, confused.

'I'm not one hundred per cent sure, but I think she once mentioned having family over there,' said Lionel.

'Well then, she's definitely not going to be back in time for the wedding,' said Mike.

'Actually, I'm not sure she's planning on coming back at all,' said Lionel.

'What makes you say that?' asked Kate.

Instead of answering, Lionel rummaged through

the wodge of papers, drew out a few that were stapled together and handed them over.

Kate flicked through them quickly while Mike leaned in to peer over her shoulder. It looked like some kind of contract with the logo of one of the large Plymouth estate agents at the top of each page. Veronica's name jumped out a couple of times as Kate scanned them. When she reached the last page, she let out a gasp. It was a photocopy of the kind of advert displayed in estate agents' windows across the country. There, in all its dilapidated glory, was a photograph of The Pebble Street Hotel.

'Yep,' said Lionel sadly, 'looks like the old girl's up for sale again.'

CHAPTER 12

'Please tell me you're joking?' said Annabel.

Kate swallowed hard, trying to battle the sick, squiggly feeling in her stomach. She'd been building up to this evening all day, driving Lou, Ethel and Sarah slowly mad. She'd been so distracted she'd kept getting orders wrong and generally wreaked havoc on their well-ordered little world.

After speaking to both Mike and Lionel at length the previous day, Kate had returned home and got straight to work calling in favours left, right and centre. By the time she'd finally gone to bed, she'd been cautiously excited that they really might be able to make this wedding happen. But now that it was time to finally explain everything to Lee and Annabel, she suddenly didn't feel quite so sure.

Mike shook his head and smiled sadly at the couple. 'No, I'm sorry. I wish we *were* joking, but it looks like

Veronica really has gone away. And, by the look on your face, I'm assuming you've not had your money back?'

'No,' said Lee, glowering and shaking his head. 'Look, I really appreciate you guys taking the time to let us know, but I think it's best if we head home and try to figure all this out.' He paused and ran his fingers through his hair, leaving the blond strands sticking out at odd angles, making him look a bit like a lost little boy. 'I guess we'd better sort out a lawyer or something.'

Kate's heart gave a sympathetic squeeze as Annabel bit her lip and reached out to grab Lee's hand. She looked so incredibly sad.

'Please stay,' said Kate gently. 'Just for a coffee. We've come up with a plan.'

Lee sighed, looking like he wanted nothing more than to hotfoot it out of Seabury as fast as he could, but Annabel looked at him pleadingly.

'Okay, fine,' he said, 'I guess there's not much we can do tonight anyway, and you guys have been so kind. I just can't see what more you can do though . . .'

'Well,' said Mike, as Ethel got to her feet to make the coffees, 'first, I should introduce everyone.' He peered around at the little group they'd gathered together. 'Lionel here is a permanent tenant of The Pebble Street Hotel - he's got an apartment on the top floor. I guess you know Ethel and Lou, and might have already met my daughter Sarah?'

Lee nodded and smiled weakly. 'In passing while we've been in here stuffing our faces!'

Mike nodded. 'Right, so . . . you asked me for an alternative quote for your reception.'

'Oh,' said Annabel, looking horrified. 'Mike, I'm really sorry, but now that Veronica's disappeared with our money, we're not going to be able to go ahead. In fact,' she stopped and took a deep breath, clearly trying to force down a swell of rising emotion, 'we've actually decided to cancel the reception altogether.'

Lee nodded sadly. 'We'll still get married as planned, but we'll just have to have a celebration when we've either managed to recoup our cash from Veronica . . . or saved up again.'

'We've got an alternative!' said Kate.

'But we can't pay you-'

'Hear us out!' grinned Mike.

Lee shrugged and sat back in his seat, but he looked defeated.

'First of all - the most important thing to you was to hold your event in the hotel, am I right?'

Annabel nodded, looking like she was pretty close to tears. 'That's why we've decided not to have it at all.'

'Well, thanks to Lionel here, we can still make that happen,' said Kate.

'But how?' said Lee. 'I don't want to be arrested for breaking and entering on my wedding night!'

Lionel chuckled. 'Well, here's the note Veronica left

me.' He passed over the crumpled bit of paper that he'd found pinned to her door.

"Sort out wedding!" huffed Lee. 'Charming.'

'I know,' said Lionel, frowning. 'But - we can just interpret that as - *make sure it goes ahead*.'

'I'm pretty sure that's not what she meant!' said Annabel, staring at it in disgust.

'No,' said Kate, 'but as Lionel's got access to the entire hotel, and technically you're fully paid up, what's to stop us using the venue?!'

'I don't know . . .' said Lee slowly, glancing at Annabel.

'What about the renovations she was going on about?' she asked.

'I'm pretty sure Ken finished up the dining room floor - but if not, I'm sure we can reach him,' said Kate.

'And the rest of the place?' asked Lee.

'I'm afraid that was another lie she told you. There isn't any work going on in the rest of the place.'

'But why would she-'

'Because it's filthy,' said Kate, her tone matter of fact. They'd all agreed to be completely upfront with the not-so-happy couple, but still - she hated this! 'Veronica clearly didn't want to put you off paying up!'

'That's not good!' said Lee, scrunching up his nose.

'Well, no, it's not,' said Lionel, 'but here's the thing. There's an old pathway that leads around the back of the building that I've been using to reach my own apartment without having to go through the rest of the hotel. There's a lovely area outside the dining room that looks out over the sea that has already been done up, and there's a set of double doors that lead to the dining room itself - which, last time I looked, was actually looking rather beautiful. You and your guests can use that!'

'But . . .'

'We've got a team together who're more than happy to blitz the kitchen, the downstairs bathrooms and the whole of the ground floor,' said Kate.

'Right . . .?' said Lee.

'You weren't intending on staying the night, were you?' asked Kate, suddenly worried. If she'd got the wrong end of the stick and they needed all the bedrooms too, then that would be one step too far for this little plan of theirs.

Annabel shook her head, looking thoughtful. 'No. We weren't planning on staying there. Everyone's got accommodation nearby sorted out already - it's only a small group of us anyway. About thirty. All we needed was a room in the hotel where we could get ready.'

'Well, I think that can be arranged in one of the other downstairs rooms,' said Lionel. 'So, what do you think?'

Lee glanced at Annabel and raised his eyebrows, then shook his head and looked back at them. 'It's really generous of you guys to offer to do this, but even with the venue sorted, that wouldn't solve the issue of a band, or food, or a cake, or decorations or . . .'

'Let us worry about all that,' said Ethel excitedly.

'But how can we!' said Annabel looking mystified. 'There's no way we could ask you to take all that on. Besides, we couldn't afford it.'

'You're after a 1940s themed do, aren't you?' said Mike.

Annabel nodded sadly. 'Yes - my dress is vintage and the men will be in uniform too. In honour of my grandma . . .' her lip quivered and Lee put his arm around her shoulders protectively.

'Well, I don't know if you're aware, but we have a rather lovely town band here in Seabury,' said Lionel. 'And a couple of those fellows have a little swing band. They do all the classics - lots of Glenn Miller and whatnot. They only play for fun, but they said they would be honoured to play at your wedding, as long as they could take some photos?'

'You're kidding?' said Lee, looking amazed.

'Nope - they've been practising in the town hall mostly, but they're excited for the chance to play for an audience!'

'That's amazing,' breathed Annabel.

'And Sarah here has agreed to do the cake,' said Mike proudly. 'She's training to be a professional baker - and as long as you don't mind her writing up an assignment about the whole thing . . .'

'It wouldn't be too big a deal,' said Sarah quietly, clearly a bit nervous at being singled out. 'I'd just need to get you to give me a bit of feedback about how I did and what you thought of the cake.'

'How much would you charge?' asked Lee.

Sarah raised her eyebrows. 'Nothing - you'd be the ones doing me a favour!' she laughed. 'I promise I won't let you down though.'

'I can vouch for Sarah,' said Kate. 'She already designs half the recipes in the cake boxes you love! And both Ethel and Lou will be on hand to help.'

Annabel's mouth was now partially open. She looked like she'd been stunned.

'As for the food,' said Mike, 'Kate and I would very much like to use your wedding as a trial run for an idea we've had for a brand new joint venture. So - if you'd be able to cover the basic costs of the ingredients, our time and services would be completely free.'

Kate glanced nervously at Annabel, only to see tears making their way quietly down her face. 'Of course,' she said quickly, 'don't worry if it's not what you want. We completely understand. We just really wanted to help if we could.'

Annabel shook her head and quickly wiped her eyes with the back of her hand. 'It's not that!' she said.

'It's *definitely* not that!' said Lee, hugging Annabel to his side. 'It's just . . . you're all so . . . *why* would you do all this for us?' he said, looking overwhelmed.

'Because this is Seabury,' said Sarah quietly. 'It's what we do.'

'Couldn't have said it better myself,' said Lionel, patting Sarah on the shoulder.

'And you really think we can pull this off in the time?' said Annabel, staring around at their motley little group.

'I think it's going to take a bit of channelling some wartime spirit,' said Ethel with a glint in her eye. 'But with the hotel empty until the big day, there's plenty of time to get in there and get it sorted out. And we've already mobilised the whole of Seabury's WI to help!'

'Lord help us,' laughed Mike, earning himself a friendly swat around the back of the head.

'What was it old Churchill said?' murmured Lionel. 'Ah yes -*victory at all costs*!'

'Hear hear!' said Mike with a grin.

CHAPTER 13

Kate had been floating around her flat in a daze all afternoon. There were a million things she knew she should be getting on with before Paula came over for the evening, but she couldn't settle to any of them. She just kept grinning to herself like an idiot at how amazing Mike was, and how determined he was to make sure Lee and Annabel had everything they wanted for their big day.

'We really do like him, don't we Stanley boy?' she said, slumping down onto the sofa and grinning over at him in his bed.

Stanley just let out a huge sigh.

'I know,' she laughed. 'No point mooning around when I'm not allowed to do anything about it, is there?'

Stanley closed his eyes.

'You know, you give the best cuddles, but you suck

at advice!' she laughed. 'Thank goodness Paula's coming over!'

She'd been over the moon when her friend had called and asked if she was free for the evening. It had been far too long since they'd had a proper catch-up. Kate was desperate to find out what was going on with her friend, but as Paula had headed off for an impromptu visit to see her mother over in Dorset, she'd had to wait longer than she'd hoped to get to the bottom of things. Even if it *was* "just hormones" like Paula had kept insisting, if they were causing her that much distress, she definitely needed some help.

Kate started to fidget again and got to her feet before she managed to pick a hole in the arm of her sofa. Paula should be here any minute.

WUFF!

Stanley lifted his head and let out another booming bark just as her doorbell rang.

'It's aunty Paula, idiot,' laughed Kate, before running downstairs to open the door for her friend.

'Kate!' Paula grinned, throwing her arms around her as if she hadn't seen her for years.

'Yay! I'm so glad you called,' said Kate holding her close. She felt thin. Far too thin.

'Well - we need to talk,' said Paula quietly, giving her a squeeze and then stepping back.

Kate did her best to ignore the knot of fear that had just formed in her stomach. Something in Paula's tone had just made a shiver go down her spine

'Oh - mum sent you this, by the way,' said Paula, brandishing a monster bottle of Baileys. 'She knows you love it and we can't stand the stuff!'

'Ohhh, thank you!' said Kate, taking the bottle. 'Come on up. Are we on a wine kind of a night or a tea kind of a night?'

'Have you got mint tea?'

'Actually, I do!' said Kate. 'Mike unearthed a jar when he was here.'

'Oh yes?' said Paula wiggling her eyebrows. Then she bit her lip. 'Sorry, I promised I wouldn't tease you about him anymore, didn't I?' she sighed.

Kate shrugged as she reached the kitchen and flicked the kettle on. Instead of the mild annoyance she usually felt when anyone teased her about Mike, she felt a kind of delighted tingle in the knowledge that he really did like her.

'I don't mind,' she said lightly.

'Well,' said Paula, peeling her leather jacket off and unwinding her scarf, 'that's definitely a change of tune!'

'I'm still not going to do anything about it,' sighed Kate, trying not to frown at just how skinny Paula looked now that she'd taken off a layer. 'Anyway - I want to hear about you first. How's your mum? Did you have a good visit?'

Paula shrugged as she watched Kate pour their drinks. 'It was a . . . *difficult* visit,' she said, following Kate through to the living room and plonking her jacket and scarf onto the arm of the sofa. She bent down to stroke Stanley, who instantly sat up and tried to lick her face, making her laugh.

Kate perched on the sofa and waited until Paula joined her, kicking off her shoes and curling her feet up underneath her like she always did.

'Why was it difficult?' asked Kate, forcing the words out. She had a feeling she didn't really want to know.

Paula took a sip of tea and then wrapped her hands around the scorching mug with a weary sigh, clearly gearing up to say something she didn't really want to.

'Is this something to do with how upset you were the other day - down on the beach?' prompted Kate.

Paula nodded. 'Yes. I'm afraid so. I got some pretty shitty news, and it's . . . it's taken me a few days to wrap my head around it.'

Kate swallowed nervously and placed her mug down on the side table, waiting for her friend to carry on.

'Kate - do you remember back in the summer when I wasn't feeling well? They thought I might have some kind of weird infection and I went for those tests?'

'Of course!' said Kate, nodding. 'But you said they didn't find anything.'

'Well, I went for some follow-ups,' she paused again, placing her mug down and rubbing her face roughly. 'Shit - I've really got to figure out a better way to tell people this,' she said.

Kate watched her, suddenly not wanting to speak - not wanting to interrupt whatever this was. She heard a scuffle and looked down only to find Stanley had abandoned his bed and come over to join them. He sat on the floor in front of Paula and plopped his head down on the sofa cushion next to her leg.

Paula smiled. 'Thanks lad,' she said, resting her hand on his head as if she was drawing courage from him. 'Kate, I'm ill,' she said gently.

'Ill?' croaked Kate.

Paula nodded. 'They were worried about something strange in those first tests. I didn't bother mentioning it because it could have been nothing. A blip. But I've been for a bunch more,' she paused again, stroking Stanley's head gently. 'I've got leukaemia.'

Kate shook her head, staring at her friend in horror. 'But - but . . .'

She shut her mouth, stopping herself from saying something stupid. She wanted to say *you can't have*, or *there's been a mistake,* or *you can fight this!* - but how would any of that help her lovely friend right now?

She slowly reached over and laid her hand on top of Paula's. 'How long have you known?' said Kate at last, her voice shaking slightly.

'Not long,' sighed Paula. 'I needed a few days to get used to the idea before telling anyone. But then on Wednesday, I'd just found out that it's the type that I can't get better from.'

'No,' said Kate, shaking her head, horrified to feel tears welling up in her eyes. They broke free, rolling hot and fast down her cheek as she fought to hold it together for her friend. She chewed the inside of her cheek, biting hard, hoping that the jolt of pain might stop her from crying and help her to focus on Paula.

She refused to make this about herself. She refused to force Paula to have to comfort her. 'No,' she said again, wishing that by saying it, she could make it true.

Paula squeezed her hand. 'I'm sorry.'

'Don't you dare apologise!' said Kate steadily, roughly wiping her tears away with her hand.

Paula nodded.

'Have they said anything about treatment? I know you said you can't get better from it, but surely-'

'There are things they can try to slow things down,' said Paula.

'When will they start?' asked Kate, feeling like these practical things might anchor her to this weird, screwed-up reality she'd suddenly landed in.

'Pretty soon,' said Paula. 'And when things get bad - towards the end-'

'Don't!' said Kate, swallowing hard.

'Please, Kate,' said Paula, turning to face her properly. 'Please. I need to be able to talk about this - I need to make it as normal as possible. I'm going to explode if I have to keep it all inside!'

Kate nodded, biting her cheek again. She could kick herself. The word had burst out of her in an instinctive reaction, but how could she be so selfish? Of course it hurt - hearing about this, but what must it be like for

Paula - living with it - knowing what would eventually happen?

'I'm sorry,' said Kate, taking Paula's other hand. 'I'm sorry. Tell me.'

Paula nodded. 'I was just going to say that when the time comes, they can make me comfortable. I'll have help to manage it.'

Kate felt the tears start up again, but she refused to look away from her friend. She nodded and squeezed her hand.

'I'm here,' she said. 'I'm here for you - for whatever you need, okay?'

Paula nodded. 'There is something I need from you.'

'Tell me,' said Kate, nodding. 'Anything!'

'I need you to help me stay me,' she said. 'All this stuff is going to pile in - hospital visits, consultants, treatment . . . fucking *end of life* plans!' she paused and let out a gasp that was half sob, half incredulous laugh. 'I need you to be my anchor - someone who'll still giggle with me over a glass of wine, watch cheesy romcoms with me, ogle cute guys with me, gossip about Seabury with me, come swimming with me!'

Kate was now crying hard, but she nodded again.

'You've got to promise me, Kate. I don't know how long I've got left. It could be years - or it could be a lot less - but the thing I'm most frightened of is people treating me differently when they find out. I've still got life to live, and I'm buggered if I'm going to waste it. Do you promise?'

Kate nodded, sniffing hard. 'I do. I promise!'

Paula sighed and a huge smile spread over her face. 'Thank you.'

Kate tried to wipe her eyes on her arm without letting go of Paula's hands, making them both giggle. It felt like the weirdest thing to do at that moment, but it felt like the medicine they both needed.

'Now then,' said Paula, sitting back and releasing Kate's hands. She grabbed her mug, gulped her tea and ruffled Stanley's ears.

Kate mopped her face and then picked up her own mug.

'On the phone, you said you had gossip for me!' said Paula.

Kate shook her head. 'That's not important,' she said. *How* could she jabber on about Veronica and the hotel and the wedding? How could she whine about Tom and ask Paula's advice about her feelings for Mike? None of it was important now.

'Oh no you don't!' laughed Paula. 'This is *exactly* what I'm talking about. Kate! Gimme the gossip! Cough up the goods! Spill! Don't make me torture you for the information.'

Kate bit her lip, fighting down a sob. 'Oh my god, you're right. I failed at the first hurdle!'

Paula shrugged. 'I think you get a bit of a grace period, given the circumstances. But I'm still me!'

Kate nodded and forced a smile onto her face.

'So - tell me everything!' said Paula gently. 'I want normal. I want to laugh. I want to help!'

Kate nodded again, took a deep breath and launched into the whole tale of Annabel and Lee's wedding and how Veronica had done a bunk with their funds. Then, with as much drama as she could inject into the story, she told her about the plan she'd concocted with Mike and the others.

'Wow!' breathed Paula as she came to the end. 'Right - you can count me in.'

'Into what?' said Kate, confused.

'Into sorting things out for this wedding, dumbass! I've taken a couple of weeks off of work - just to get my head around things and get a plan in place. I'd *love* to help!'

'Really?' asked Kate, looking doubtful.

'Hell yes! I might not be firing on all cylinders, but I'd love to be involved.'

'Okay then - count yourself well and truly roped in!' said Kate with a smile.

'So . . . erm . . .' said Paula, suddenly looking uneasy.

'What?' asked Kate. 'Talk to me about anything. I mean it.'

Paula snorted. 'Okay - you asked for it. My question is - why haven't you snogged Mike Pendle's face off yet?!'

Kate let out a surprised giggle. 'Well, as this is a night of being completely honest with each other . . . it's getting more and more difficult not to!'

'Yay!'

'No, not *yay*. Seriously. I keep feeling like I'm falling for him, and there's nothing I can do about it.'

'Eh? There's *everything* you can do about it!' said Paula, practically jumping up and down on the sofa in excitement, making Stanley wag his tail.

'No,' said Kate. 'Like I told him, now's not the time. Not with all the nonsense with Tom still up in the air. I can't just dive into something new - it wouldn't be fair to him.'

'Well,' said Paula with a frown, 'I think recent events mean that I'm newly qualified to tell you this - life's too short for all that rubbish!'

Kate felt the smile drop off her face.

'I promise not to keep using this card,' smirked Paula, 'but just this once, let me tell you that you deserve to be happy *right now*. It's what I'm planning to do - and I think you should too.'

'But-'

'No buts Kate! Don't let time just keep passing you by. It's finite. Do the things you want to do, love the people you want to love. Stop waiting for the perfect moment - because no moment is more perfect than right now.'

CHAPTER 14

It had been a couple of days since her evening with Paula, and Kate still felt like her well-ordered little world was inside out and upside down. She'd cried herself to sleep that night after Ryan had picked Paula up - but that was all she was willing to give herself for now. Kate absolutely refused to go into mourning when Paula was still right there - alive, kicking and needing her support.

In a way, it was a godsend that she had so much to do. Planning for the wedding meant that she was dropping into bed late, so exhausted that she was practically passing out instead of falling asleep. Her days were non-stop, working with Mike to get all the details ironed out on top of keeping The Sardine up and running.

She knew, deep down, that it would probably be a good idea for her to take a bit of time to digest what was happening and work through the news that one of her favourite people in the entire world was going to be facing this huge, sad struggle. That her best friend was - at some point - going to disappear from her life forever. But she just couldn't. Not yet.

The worst moments had been the quiet ones when she was able to take a breather and think. For that reason, she was very glad to be handing the delivery round over to Lou for the next few weeks. The long, quiet ride gave her brain way too much time to chase itself down grief-filled rabbit holes.

Sadly, she couldn't escape from *all* the difficult moments. Paula had asked Kate if she'd be willing to share the news with Lou, Ethel and Sarah for her. She wasn't quite ready for her diagnosis to become common knowledge just yet, but as she was planning to help them out with the wedding, she'd decided that it would be best for Kate's little team to know what was going on.

After taking a couple of days to wrap her own head around things, Kate had finally bitten the bullet and gathered the trio together after closing time. Right now, she was feeling like the worst person ever for making three of her favourite people so very sad.

'Well, she's a brave lass - no mistaking that!' said Ethel, letting out a shuddering sigh. 'I really admire her attitude. I do feel for poor Ryan though, I wonder how he's doing?'

'Paula said he's being his usual, sweet self,' said Kate,

with a soft smile. 'He'll be there for her through thick and thin, just like he's always been.'

Where Paula had always been a whirlwind of wild-swimming, wine-drinking, giggly energy, her husband was a gentle, easy-going soul - dedicated to books, reading and pots of tea. They were one of those couples you'd never have put together in a million years, and yet their marriage had been rock solid ever since their "I do" moment just after they'd graduated from uni.

'Well, we'll have to make sure we're there for him too,' said Lou, her face sombre.

Ethel nodded and patted her on the back. Lou might not have lived in Seabury long, but she was one of those people that just seemed to belong there.

'I wish there was something we could do to help her,' said Sarah, wiping under her eyes with a piece of kitchen roll, trying to remove the mascara smudges from the tears she'd been unable to hold back.

Paula and Kate had discussed at length whether they should tell Sarah or not, but in the end, they'd decided that - provided Mike agreed - it would be kinder to let her know and support her, rather than risk her accidentally finding out when Seabury's gossip-mill kicked into gear.

'There is,' said Kate, putting her arm around Sarah's shoulders. 'It's what she asked me to do - and you guys can help too.'

'What. Anything!' said Sarah earnestly.

'Well . . .' Kate wracked her brains for the best way to paraphrase their tear-soaked conversation, 'she's going to be going through a lot - hospital and treatments and all that. She wants my help - *our* help - to still be the Paula we know and love.'

'I don't understand,' said Sarah, frowning.

'She wants *normal*, love,' said Ethel, raising her eyebrows at Kate, checking that she'd got this right.

'Exactly,' said Kate, nodding. 'She wants to giggle and have fun and do things like help us with this wedding. She still wants you to tell her rude jokes and share news about college with her like you always do when she comes in here.'

'But how does that help?' said Sarah, sounding mildly desperate.

'Because the thing she's dreading most is people treating her differently,' said Kate. 'Paula wants to enjoy every second she can. I think having a bunch of people she can rely on to treat her the same - no matter what she's going through, or how much she changes outwardly - is going to give her a boost when things get difficult.'

Sarah nodded. 'It doesn't seem like much though . . .'

Kate smiled at her. 'To Paula, it means everything.'

Sarah nodded again, grabbed Kate's hand and squeezed it. 'The four of us can be here for each other too, *and* for Paula and Ryan.'

'Yeah boss,' said Lou, frowning at Kate across the

table. 'Don't forget that we're all here for you too, okay?'

Ethel and Sarah both nodded vigorously as Kate swallowed hard and smiled at them, trying to push her emotions back into place. She was so grateful, but right now it was time to get her practical head back on before she lost it completely.

'Right!' she said, letting out a long breath, 'it's going to have to be a case of divide and conquer over the next few days to get everything done! Lou - are you certain you're happy to take on Trixie for me?'

Lou nodded eagerly. 'Yup - and the morning prep for the deliveries too.'

'Fab!' said Kate gratefully. 'Sarah - are you still happy to do the cake for Lee and Annabel now you've had a couple of days to think about it?'

Sarah nodded, staring hard at the table.

'Brilliant! You're very welcome to use the kitchen in The Sardine any time after closing if you need to work on ideas or trial runs - though your dad's place has got lots more space and is probably easier for you!'

'I've got some sketches I'm working on,' said Sarah. 'I'd love to bring them in and see what you guys think before I show them to Annabel?'

Ethel and Lou nodded, looking excited.

'Happy to help with anything, if you need me too,' said Ethel.

'Yep, me too,' said Lou.

'Not that you'll need either of us,' laughed Ethel.

'And are you still happy to lead the charge with the WI over at the hotel?' Kate asked Ethel. 'I'll help as much as I can in the evenings, but if you guys can get the place clean, I can man the fort here while you're all out on your missions!'

'Happy with that!' said Ethel. 'Then when we've got the place smelling a bit better, I'll take over from you in here for a few days Kate, and that should free you up to work your magic with Mike!'

Kate smiled, but dropped her head in her hands as all three of them started on their usual round of *nudge, nudge, wink, wink, Kate lurves Mike!*

'For heaven sakes, you three,' she sighed.

'Ah come on,' said Lou, wiggling her eyebrows.

'Yeah - I had to put up with it for years about Charlie!' laughed Ethel.

'No offence Ethel,' said Sarah, 'but you two ended up as the cutest couple ever . . . so . . .'

'Oh hush, you,' giggled Ethel. 'But that does remind me - Charlie told me to pass on that he's available to help in any way you need him for the wedding - or anything else. Even if it's just to look after Stanley or walk him while you're so busy.'

'You've got a good one, there, Ethel!' said Kate with a smile.

'Don't I know it, love!' she beamed. 'Just don't tell him - I'll never live it down!'

This really was the most spectacular view. Veronica might be a conniving, bitter woman, but she'd been quite right to think that people would give a lot to celebrate their wedding day out here.

Kate had arrived early for her meeting with Mike at The Pebble Street Hotel, so she'd decided to sit out on the newly renovated area outside the dining room. The low, autumn sunshine on her face combined with the gentle lapping of the sea below was exquisite. She'd meant to run through her plans while she waited but instead, she'd just been sitting here, gazing dreamily out over The King's Nose, and across the bay to where the lighthouse stood sentry out on the point.

Her picnic up there with Mike felt like months ago, not days, and she wished that they could be up there right now, with the fresh breeze blowing off the sea and Stanley snuffling around them while they tucked into a picnic like last time. And maybe, just maybe - if he asked her on a date again - this time she'd say yes.

Paula's words about living for the moment kept echoing around her head. She knew her friend was right, but on the other hand, she still hadn't heard anything back from Philip about what Tom was up to. It had been a relief just to know that he was on the case, though, and he'd promised her – if nothing else – that she wouldn't have to wait too long for a resolution.

She hated all this waiting - but if she was being totally honest, ever since Paula's news it had shifted into the background a bit. Still - could she really think of moving on without making sure that The Sardine was safe?

The thing was, every time she saw Mike, she just wanted to run her hands through his hair and cuddle into him. Considering they were now working together to make sure Lee and Annabel's big day was as special as they could make it, it was getting harder and harder to ignore how she felt. And given the number of times she'd caught him gazing at her when he thought she wasn't looking, she was pretty sure he was in the same boat. At least – a little bit.

'Penny for them?' came a quiet voice from behind her.

Kate smiled without turning. 'Hey Mike!' she said gently.

'Hey yourself. Sorry I'm late,' he said, dropping onto the wooden bench next to her and staring out at the sea. 'Where's our boy?'

'Stanley?' she asked. 'Charlie took him up to the allotments for a run around while he went to fetch some tools.'

'That's good. You know he's invited to the wedding, right?'

'He is?' laughed Kate.

Mike nodded. 'Lee and Annabel have issued a general invitation to all of us who're helping - but Lee added a special mention for Stanley - I think he's fallen for him!'

Kate grinned. 'Not the only one, eh?'

Mike smiled. 'My first four-legged love,' he laughed.

'Right,' said Kate, sitting up and trying to stop herself from staring at Mike like a love-sick idiot, 'shall we run through where we're up to with everything so far?

'Erm . . . before we get onto all things wedding . . . can I ask you something a bit awkward?'

Kate raised her eyebrows at him. Holy crap - was he about to save her a job and ask her out again?

'It's about Sarah,' he said with a slight frown.

'Oh,' said Kate, trying to ignore the fact that her heart just sank a little bit. 'Of course, what's up?'

'Well - that's what I was going to ask you,' said Mike, running his hand around the back of his neck and looking decidedly uncomfortable. 'She's been pretty quiet recently - ever since the news about Aunty Sally.'

'Well, that's to be expected, I guess,' said Kate.

'Yeah - but I was wondering what happened at that last staff meeting you had? I know you talked about Paula - and that must have been incredibly difficult for you all,' he paused and took Kate's hand, giving it a squeeze.

Kate simply nodded, but she didn't move her hand away.

'But . . . did anything else happen?'

Kate frowned. 'Not really. We *did* talk about Paula - and although it was really hard, we discussed the ways we could all be there for her. Sarah was upset, but I think she understood.'

'But nothing else?'

Kate shrugged. 'Erm - I just made sure that everyone was happy with what we're all doing to keep things running while we're busy . . . and I double-checked Sarah's still happy to make the wedding cake - which she was. Why?'

'Since she got back, she's gone from quiet to angry and snappy. I know she's a teen and everything, but it's really not like her!'

'Blimey,' said Kate, frowning at him. 'Well . . . I guess it could have been the news about Paula?'

Mike shrugged. 'Maybe . . .'

'Or perhaps stuff around your Aunty . . . or . . . maybe having to do this cake is actually too much for her?'

'I guess it could be,' said Mike, looking uncertain. 'But she was really excited about that. She's been doodling pages of ideas ever since we asked her.' He stopped and let out a huge sigh. 'All I know is that there's something really wrong, and whenever I ask her what's up, she just bites my head off.'

'Hmm . . . I hate to say it, but that can be pretty standard practise for a teenage girl,' chuckled Kate, her mind wandering back to her own handful of scary hormonal outbursts.

'I get what you're saying, but . . . this is something more. Something different.'

Kate frowned at him and then, realising she was still holding his hand, quickly gave it a squeeze and let go. 'I'll see if I can sound her out a bit if I get the opportunity,' she said, getting to her feet.

'Thanks Kate!' he said, following suit. 'And you?' he asked, suddenly. 'How are you doing with all of this?'

Kate traced the crack in the brand new paving slabs with her toe, wishing she could disappear between them. 'I'm just glad we're busy,' she said, her voice giving her away with a little wobble.

Mike nodded. 'If you need me, I'm here, okay?'

Kate nodded and screwed her hands into tight fists at her side, digging her fingernails in hard – whether it was in a bid to stop herself from crying or from throwing herself at him and kissing his face off - she wasn't quite sure.

'Right,' she said, taking a step towards the double doors into the dining room, 'I think it's time to whip this wedding into shape.'

CHAPTER 15

'I can't believe how much they've already done!' said Kate, her jaw dropping as they stood together in the middle of the newly pristine kitchen. There wasn't any sign of the washing-up mountain, the grimy, fat-stained backsplash or the stinking slops bucket. Everything had been emptied out, scrubbed to within an inch of its life and then left in apple-pie order. This was now a kitchen that Kate could imagine a professional chef hard at work in.

'You know,' said Mike, looking around, 'this country would be in a much better shape if we just let Ethel and Seabury's WI run it!'

'Now there's a terrifying thought!' laughed Kate. 'But this is perfect, isn't it? It will be far easier to prep everything for the wedding in here rather than trying to do it all over at The Sardine or your place. It's enough of a battle keeping the cafes running as well as making sure this bun fight goes off without a hitch!'

'Spot on,' agreed Mike. 'I know Annabel has completely fallen for the idea of everyone helping themselves to food from the back of Trixie - so we might have to look at fitting up some kind of display for the trailer. Any thoughts?'

Kate glanced around her, her mind racing. 'Ken,' she said with a flash of inspiration. 'The guy who did the repairs to the floor in the dining room. I bet he would help or would know someone who could.'

'Think he'd be up for it?'

Kate shrugged. 'He gave me his card when he came in for lunch, so I can always call and find out. He was a really nice chap.'

They wandered out of the kitchen and into the hallway, which now smelled of polish rather than cabbage. 'Huh!' said Kate, 'the carpet's a different colour.'

'Yes - amazing what a spot of hoovering does!' laughed Lionel, striding towards them from upstairs.

'Hi!' said Kate with a grin.

'Tour of inspection?' he asked.

Kate nodded. 'Sort of. We just wanted to see where we're up to - Lee and Annabel are popping down in a bit for a look around.'

'Jolly good,' said Lionel. 'Oh - by the way, I was talking to Ethel when she was here - and we were wondering if the breakfast lounge might make a nice space for the happy couple to have as a kind of dressing room to relax in away from everything?'

'It's so grim in the breakfast lounge though,' sighed Kate, thinking of the dregs of cold coffee and congealed cornflakes awaiting them.

Lionel shook his head. 'Look again!' He led them along to the lounge and threw open the door with a flourish.

'Blimey,' exclaimed Mike wandering in, 'the cleaning fairies have been in here too!'

Kate took one step in and stopped dead. 'Okay - Ethel for president!' she laughed.

'Actually, I should tell you that Paula was most definitely in charge of this bit,' chuckled Lionel.

'That figures,' said Kate, blinking hard as she felt a couple of rogue tears appear in the corners of her eyes. Not wanting the others to notice this sudden swell of emotion, she took several steps into the space, facing away from them in the pretence of taking it all in.

The manky little tables and spindly chairs were gone - along with the echoes of breakfasts long past. The room somehow looked larger and cosier at the same time. The windows had been cleaned and the soft autumn light flooded in.

Kate longed to throw herself onto one of the two squashy sofas that had appeared as if by magic . . . but she just about managed to stop herself. She had a sneaking suspicion that if she lay down right now, the siren-call of a nap might prove to be way too tempting.

'So,' said Lionel, 'Paula got us to roll this massive old carpet back, then a team of them scrubbed the floor and gave it some kind of treatment. When that was dry, they went to work on the carpet too - I never knew it was such a handsome one if I'm honest - it's always been too covered in bits of breakfast before!'

Mike shook his head in wonder. 'You know, I'd be happy to actually get married in here, it's that nice,' he said. 'You could just imagine those lovely windows making the perfect backdrop, and you could have the chairs here, and a stand of flowers over there and . . .' he petered out as Kate turned to him with her eyebrows raised in amusement. 'You know what I mean!' he added, clearing his throat and turning a beautiful berry red.

Lionel chuckled. '*I* do! Now that you can actually see out through the windows, look at that view!' he said, pointing through the great arches of glass. You could see right to the other side of Seabury from here, all the way to where the allotments lay on the slopes of the far hill.

'Where did all this gorgeous furniture come from though?' said Kate. 'It must have cost a fortune - I feel like I've stepped into an Austen adaptation!'

Lionel shook his head. 'Nope - it's all from the hotel,' he said, patting an ornate wooden bureau. 'Paula, Charlie and I went for a nose around upstairs. Paula chose the bits she wanted for in here, and Charlie and I - with a little bit of help from a couple of the other chaps from the allotments - brought it all down for her.'

'Sounds like Paula,' Kate laughed. The emotion swelled in her chest again, but this time it was pure pride. She'd turned the room into an elegant, cosy place to spend time - and Kate was excited to let Lee and Annabel see it. 'I think they're going to love it!'

'Me too,' said Mike. 'But hearing you mention "upstairs" has just made me think - I reckon we'd better rope the stairs off somehow. It's one thing letting the guests wander around down here where it's all been cleaned, but upstairs is . . .'

'Yucky?' said Lionel.

'Erm . . . yep!' said Mike.

'Well, it's not quite as bad now. A handful of over-enthusiastic WI ladies and a fleet of Henry hoovers have had a good rampage up there since you last saw it.'

'You're joking,' said Kate. 'We didn't mean for them to take on the entire bloomin' hotel!'

Lionel shrugged. 'I overheard Doreen from the Post Office tell Celia Jones that she wouldn't be able to sleep unless she did something about it.'

Mike snorted. 'I might have to tell Doreen that my place is in a state too - just to see if she'll come around once a week and hoover for me!'

Kate smirked at him. 'So, how far did they get?'

'The whole lot,' grinned Lionel. 'I mean, not like down here, where everything - including the door-knobs - has been polished. But everything's been hoovered and dusted, and the public bathrooms have been scrubbed too. If we just close the bedroom doors and turn a key in the locks, then it won't matter if the guests decide to take a wander around, will it?'

'When this is done,' said Mike, 'we're going to hold a special event at my place and invite everyone for free coffees and cream teas to say thank you.'

'They'd like that,' said Kate with a soft smile. 'Though be prepared for plenty of critique on your jam and the lightness of your scones.'

'Ha - no chance,' he chuckled, 'I'll rope Ethel into making them for me!'

'Poaching my staff now, are we Mr Pendle?' she laughed.

'It's not poaching if we're working together, is it?' he said with his eyes twinkling.

'So what are you going to name this little joint events-venture of yours then?' asked Lionel.

'Frothy Sardine?' said Mike, trying to keep his face straight as Kate gave him a hefty dig in the ribs.

'Um – eeew!' laughed Kate, shaking her head.

'You know what keeps bothering me,' said Lionel.

'What?' asked Kate.

'Well, you're doing all this work – and so many people are getting involved to make it happen - and it's all benefitting Veronica. It just doesn't seem right, somehow.'

'How's it benefitting Veronica?' said Mike. 'I don't know about you guys, but I'm doing this for Lee and

Annabel - and us a little bit too,' he shot a sly grin at Kate.

'Well,' said Lionel, 'Pebble Street's going to be in a much better state when all this is over - and that's only going to help her sell it, isn't it?'

'Maybe think about it like this,' said Kate gently, 'hopefully it will bring a new owner who really cares about the old place. Someone who'll love the hotel as much as you do. If that happens - then it's got to be worth it, hasn't it?'

Lionel nodded, though she could see his mind was still working under those frowning, bushy brows. She gently took his arm and smiled up at him. 'It'll work out, Lionel. I know it will.'

'So - what do you think?' asked Mike.

Kate watched Annabel and Lee as they stared around the dining room and then back out through the open double doors towards the sea.

'I think you are my new heroes,' said Annabel, turning to them with tears in her eyes. 'You have no idea how much this means to me. I know we didn't see it at its worst, but I can see how much work you've already done in here. I just . . . I . . .'

Kate stepped forward and instinctively put her arm around Annabel as her chin quivered. She understood how much a place could mean when it held treasured memories of someone you loved so dearly. It was like the way the old lighthouse made her feel closer to her lovely dad – like he was still there with her.

'I'm so glad you like it,' said Kate. 'And when it's all decorated and Trixie's here with the food, it should look quite special.'

'I love the outdoor space,' said Lee.

'Well,' said Lionel, 'Ethel's chap, Charlie, is coming down later on today. He's got the green fingers, so all those new planters will be filled up. He said he's got just the thing to plant in there to give you some colour for your big day, as well as some huge tubs of autumn crocuses that are about to bloom.'

'Crocuses were nan's favourite!' said Annabel, leaning her head on Kate's shoulder.

Kate smiled over at Mike, and she saw his shoulders relax a little.

'Charlie's also going to clear the outdoor passage like we talked about so your guests can come around the back like you asked,' said Kate, 'but, as the WI ladies have done such a fab job, we can actually open up the whole ground floor for you - and you can use the main entrance too.'

'I still can't believe you've done all this for us,' said Lee. 'Thank you so much!'

Mike grinned. 'It's nothing.'

'Erm - nope!' laughed Lee.

'Okay, it's *something* . . . but we're enjoying it, aren't we?' said Mike.

Kate smiled at him and nodded. Yes, even though her life should feel like it was crumbling at the seams right now, this was definitely something she was enjoying.

'Oh,' she said, 'I forgot to tell you. My friend Paula, who's been helping out, knows Emmy Martin who owns Grandad Jim's Flower Farm over in Little Bamton.'

'Wow,' said Annabel, 'what a wonderful job!'

'I know,' said Kate, 'I thought that too! Anyway - I know Veronica was meant to be sorting out that side of things – and I don't think she even tried to get flowers booked. Emmy does buckets of mixed, cut flowers and we figured - if you still wanted some flowers in here - we could get our crack team of WI flower arrangers to work their magic with a couple of them?'

'Yes,' said Lee, wrapping his arm around Annabel's shoulders as she went to stand next to him. 'Yes please. And if she's got dahlias, it's a triple yes please.'

Kate raised her eyebrows in delight. She'd expected Annabel to be the one to jump at the flowers.

'Lee's a sucker for flowers,' laughed Annabel.

'And thank goodness I'm marrying a woman who likes buying them for me.'

Kate watched as Lee gathered Annabel into the sweetest kiss, then without meaning to, her eyes drifted over to Mike, only to find that he was staring at her, and the look he was giving her took her breath away.

Lionel let out a huge sigh. 'Young love,' he said. Kate nodded and glanced at him, but instead of watching the canoodling couple, he was looking between her and Mike with misty eyes.

'Don't *you* start!' laughed Kate, making Mike snort with laughter.

CHAPTER 16

Kate stretched and let out a huge yawn, promptly echoed by Stanley in his bed. Ethel and Lou had booted her out of the cafe for the last few hours. The weather was so bad that there was barely anyone around, so she'd taken them up on the offer of a couple of hours to herself. She'd promised them she was going to have a nap and chill out, but in reality, she'd just spent most of the afternoon making sure that everything was ready for Lee and Annabel's big day.

She'd called Emmy at Grandad Jim's Flower Farm, and when she'd told her the story, Emmy had given her a whopping discount. Mike had already ordered several cases of sparkling wine from his contact at the vineyard just outside of Little Bamton, so she called them to ask if they could pop in to collect them on the same trip.

Her last call had been to Ken - who'd greeted her like an old friend, waxed lyrical about how much he'd enjoyed his lunch at The Sardine, and then happily agreed to make her a speedy display for Trixie. The only proviso was that she'd cater his fortieth wedding anniversary the following year.

It was only when she'd ended the call that Kate had realised she might not even be the owner of The Sardine in a year's time. The thought had been enough to puncture the happy bubble she'd managed to surround herself with, and suddenly she needed to get out of the flat.

'Right, Stanley lad!' she said, getting up and wincing as her spine let out a series of snaps, crackles and pops from sitting still for far too long. 'Let's grab a walk and then take Trixie over to the hotel.'

Deep down, she knew that Trixie would be able to navigate the newly-cleared passageway around the back of the hotel with no trouble, but she didn't want to leave such an important element untested. She'd mentioned it to Mike earlier, and he'd suggested that Kate wheel Trixie over there to do a quick walk-through - just to make sure and set her mind at ease.

The minute she grabbed a jacket and Stanley's lead, he hopped straight out of his bed and followed her downstairs, letting out a massive yawn.

As she expected, The Sardine's blinds were down and by the looks of things everyone had headed home for the evening. Making sure that all three of her staff had their own key was the best thing Kate had ever done. It took the pressure off having to be there for opening and closing time every day - even if it was a bit weird not being one hundred per cent sure who was still pottering around downstairs when she was up in her flat.

'Ah bollocks!' she breathed as she turned towards the yard where Trixie was tucked up for the night. There, blocking the entrance, was a posh estate car. 'Hang on a minute, I recognise you,' she said with a frown.

She stared around her but there was no sign of anyone, let alone Mike or Sarah. She sighed and fiddled around in her pocket for her phone.

'Pick up, Mike,' she muttered as it rang. 'Come on, come on, come on. Balls!' she said as it went to voice mail. 'Okay. Change of plan. Come on Stanley, we're off to New York Froth!'

It wasn't quite the chilled, relaxing walk she'd been hoping to have along the seafront. Kate was quietly seething. It always rubbed her up the wrong way when anyone parked across the entrance to the yard. For one thing, it had signs all over it indicating that the gates were in constant use. Yes, she *knew* that it was after closing time - but with that idiot parked there, it meant she wouldn't be able to get Trixie out and over to the hotel as she'd planned.

She blew out a frustrated breath. Of course, this was worse than some random, thoughtless visitor blocking her in - because she was pretty sure that was Sienna's car. Mike's ex. Otherwise known as the evil cow-bag who'd run her and Stanley off the road earlier in the summer. The accident had resulted in Stanley getting injured - and Kate swearing an oath never to let the woman off the hook for hurting her boy.

By the time they reached New York Froth, she was out of breath and in a decided huff. Kate impatiently hit Mike's doorbell.

'Come on,' she muttered. She knew it was totally unfair on him, but if his ex was in town, he was the most likely person to know where she was. Or had she got this very wrong? Perhaps Mike had borrowed the car for some reason, and parked it there because . . . why? For some kind of strange joke? Or because he was in a rush . . . or maybe . . . maybe he was at the hotel?

Stanley let out a massive sigh and sat on Kate's foot, making her laugh. 'I know, boy,' she chuckled. 'I'm an idiot. He's clearly not here. Let's try calling him again!'

She yanked out her mobile and pulled Mike's number up again. This time he answered on the second ring.

'Hey Kate!' he said, and she could hear the smile in his voice.

'Hey yourself! Where are you?'

'Oh, I'm . . . er . . . why? Where are you?' he said.

Kate raised her eyebrows. 'I'm outside your place, looking for you,' she laughed.

'Oh! Sorry, I'm not in town at the moment.'

'Bugger.'

'Sorry?'

'There's a bit of a situation. I didn't realise Sienna's in town?'

'Huh? You've lost me!'

'Your ex-wife . . .?'

'Yes, I know who Sienna is, unfortunately,' laughed Mike.

'Well, her car's currently blocking Trixie's yard. I thought maybe you'd borrowed it or something, but-'

'No, not me,' said Mike quickly. 'But it can't be Sienna - she's miles away. Kate are you *sure* it's not just some other random person with the same car?' he asked.

Kate was suddenly intensely grateful that he couldn't see her as the blush started somewhere in her toes and quickly made its way right the way up to her face.

'I guess it could be,' she muttered.

She heard Mike let out a chuckle.

'Sorry,' she said. 'I just saw it and instantly saw red!'

'Oh trust me - I understand that better than you'd ever imagine!' he laughed.

'It's cocked up my plans for taking Trixie over to the hotel tonight, though,' she sighed.

'Well - maybe just take a night off?' he said lightly. 'I reckon you've earned it.'

'Thanks boss!' she laughed. For a long second, Kate

was tempted to ask him if he'd like to meet up for a drink ... but then, that could lead to-

'Kate, you still there?'

'Oh, uh, yeah - sorry.'

'I've got to head off - I should be back in town in about an hour or so.'

'Okay. Erm. Okay, cool. I'll catch you tomorrow then?'

'Tomorrow,' said Mike.

Stanley stared at her as she slipped her mobile back into her pocket. 'What?' she said, grinning down at him.

Stanley let out another sigh.

'I know. I'm a wuss. I'm nowhere near as brave as Aunty Paula. She'd have just asked him out already. Anyway - looks like it's just you and me, old boy. Come on!'

'Huh,' she said, drawing to a halt on the pavement opposite The Sardine. She was sure the lights had been off when she'd passed the cafe on her way out, but now she could see light sneaking around the edges of the blinds. Perhaps one of the others had forgotten something and popped back in. 'Come on lad, let's check it out.'

Casting the shiny estate car a filthy look, Kate let Stanley off his lead but suddenly paused at the cafe door, certain that she could hear raised voices coming from inside. She glanced down at Stanley, and his raised ears and the fact that he was staring at the door in alarm seemed to confirm it. What she wasn't expecting to hear from him was a grumble low down in his throat. It was very rare for her big softy to make that kind of sound!

She listened intently for a moment, but completely unable to make out the words, she pushed her way inside.

'Sarah?' she said. The young girl had her back to the door, and it looked like she was busy with something over on the stove.

'Kate?' Sarah whipped around, and Kate let out a shriek. Sarah's eyes were red and swollen from crying and her face was all puffy.

'What's wrong, sweetheart?

'What's wrong is that she is being a baby,' came a hard, angry voice from behind Kate.

Kate spun back to the little table in the corner. A woman was sitting there, glaring at her. She hadn't spotted her on her way in because she'd been so focused on Sarah. She looked a lot like her young member of staff - but at the same time, nothing like her. She didn't have the warmth dancing behind her eyes, or the wide smile Sarah had clearly inherited from her father.

'You must be Sienna,' said Kate without an ounce of warmth or welcome.

'And who are you? We're having a private conversation.'

'This is Kate's place,' said Sarah quietly.

'Don't interrupt!' snapped Sienna, and Kate saw Sarah flinch. Before she could react, however, Stanley let out a deep growl and came to stand directly in front of Sienna, his hackles raised and his tail completely still.

'It's okay boy,' said Kate, her voice low and gentle. She'd never seen him like this before and the last thing she needed was for him to go for the woman – even though she wouldn't blame him in the slightest.

'Get your dog away from me,' said Sienna coldly.

'I suggest you get yourself away from my dog,' said Kate, gently laying her hand on Stanley's collar and clipping the lead she was still carrying back in place. She trusted Stanley implicitly - but he had a strong protective streak. Given that Sarah was currently a shaking mess, she wasn't surprised that it had gone into overdrive.

'Come on lad,' she said, practically dragging him away so that he was over nearer to the kitchen. 'What's going on, Sarah?' she said, desperately wanting to put an arm around the girl, but unable to get Stanley to budge far enough to do so.

Sarah looked at her, tears still cascading down her face.

'What's going on is that she's finally seeing sense and coming away with me.'

Kate glanced at Sarah as her sobbing seemed to double.

'Have you talked to Mike about this?' Kate asked, doing her best not to sound threatening.

'Huh, so you're the new bit on the side are you?' she spat. 'No. I don't need to talk to your pathetic boyfriend to take my daughter away. She's being wasted here. I've found her a place at a prestigious culinary college in Paris. She will learn from the best.'

'Paris?' said Kate, desperately trying to catch up. 'She's still got almost two years to finish where she is.'

'She dropped out,' said Sienna with a sneer.

'You made me,' sobbed Sarah.

Stanley strained at his lead and Kate braced herself in case he was about to make a dash for Sienna, but then relaxed as he struggled to get to Sarah instead. She let go of his lead so that he could dash around the corner, no doubt to sit on Sarah's feet.

'I did not *make* you,' said Sienna. 'You agreed that Paris would be good.'

'*One day,*' sobbed Sarah. 'I said maybe *one day!*'

'Grow up. You've got the money to do it now. Stop wasting your life here.'

'Okay,' said Kate, 'that's enough. Sarah, love, do you want me to call your dad?'

'He's not home,' said Sarah, turning to her. 'That's why I came to yours. I don't want to go!'

'You're not going anywhere,' said Kate. She turned towards Sienna. 'I'd like you to get out of my cafe now, please. You can talk this through with Mike, but I'm not leaving you alone with Sarah.'

'Oh, be quiet, you sappy bitch!'

'Get out, or I'm calling the police,' growled Kate, moving around the counter and putting an arm around Sarah. She could feel her quivering all over and it made her anger towards this awful woman swell even further. 'And move your car, or I'll have you towed.'

Sienna got to her feet and moved a couple of paces towards them but came to an abrupt halt as Stanley dashed out of the kitchen with a warning growl.

'You're as big a loser as your father,' she spat at Sarah, not taking her eyes off of Stanley. 'I can't believe I wasted so much energy on you. You've got a day to apologise. After that - I'm cancelling Paris – not that you'll ever make anything of yourself anyway.'

Kate watched Sienna turn on her heel and storm out of the cafe. The minute the door closed behind her mother, Sarah dissolved into a sobbing wreck, her arms around Kate's middle as her tears soaked into the shoulder of her jumper.

Kate held her close for what felt like hours, though in reality, it was probably only about five minutes. But there was no way she was letting go until Sarah's breathing calmed down and her tears had eased up.

When Sarah finally stepped back, doing her best to wipe her face while Stanley desperately tried to lick her hands, Kate let out a long breath. She quickly nipped over to the door and turned the key in the lock.

It wasn't that she was afraid of Sienna - but she needed Sarah to feel completely safe while they figured out what to do next.

'I'm going to give your dad a call,' she said.

Sarah nodded, sinking down onto the floor and wrapping her arms around Stanley. Kate had a sneaking suspicion that she was crying again. She quickly grabbed her mobile and called Mike.

'I'm feeling very popular right now,' came his booming laugh.

'Where are you?' said Kate. She did her best to keep her voice calm, not wanting to alarm him - or Sarah, for that matter.

'Why?' he said, and she could hear the instant worry in his voice. 'What's wrong.'

'It's Sarah,' she said, not quite sure how to tell him what she'd just walked in on. 'That car *was* Sienna's.'

'Oh God, what's she done?' he said, and she could hear the anger already building in his voice.

'Can you come straight to The Sardine?'

'I'll be there in ten minutes.'

'Great. Give me a call when you're outside - I've got the door locked.'

CHAPTER 17

'Well,' said Mike, handing Kate a glass of brandy and then throwing himself down into the sofa next to her, 'she's stopped crying and Stanley's practically in bed with her!' He gave her a weak smile and took a sip of his drink.

'He can stay with her tonight,' said Kate smiling back.

'Thank you. I swear that dog is the best therapy there is!'

'I don't think your ex would agree,' muttered Kate, 'it's a miracle Stanley didn't go for her. I've never seen him quite so protective.'

'Sarah's basically terrified of Sienna. Stanley was just protecting a scared pup.'

Kate nodded. 'I don't quite get what I walked in on,' she said. She didn't want to interrogate Mike, but equally, she was desperate to know that Sarah was safe and wouldn't be forced into something against her will.

Mike sighed. 'I think Sarah and I have quite a bit of talking to do when she's calmed down, but reading between the lines, Sienna's somehow found out that Sarah's inherited a bunch of money from Aunty Sally. I guarantee she will have already blown through what she got in the divorce, so I'm guessing she figured she'd like to get her hands on it.'

'*What?!*' squeaked Kate.

'Mmm,' growled Mike. 'She's been in far more regular contact with Sarah since the news. I didn't say anything because I know Sarah's been having a hard time and I figured that maybe she needed her mum. I mean - there's a first time for everything, right? As it turns out - Sienna *is* the hard time she's been having.'

'Oh my goodness,' said Kate, absolutely horrified that someone would do that to their own child.

'Yeah. Anyway - Sienna's been in town for several days now - hounding Sarah. Sounds like her and her boyfriend were after an all-expenses-paid year in Paris courtesy of Sarah while they "looked after her".'

'You don't think she would have actually tried to force her to leave, do you?' said Kate, feeling sick at the thought.

Mike frowned. 'Sienna's quite full-on . . .'

'Yeah, I noticed,' muttered Kate.

'Let's just say, I'm really glad you were there. Thank you.'

'I'd do anything for either of you,' said Kate, reaching out and resting her hand on his. Mike turned to her and locked his eyes on hers.

'Same, Kate.'

Kate swallowed. This wasn't the moment.

'What is it?' he asked quietly, not taking his eyes off her.

Kate could feel herself growing red, but she couldn't look away. 'It's not the moment,' she said out loud, shaking her head slightly. Right now, she wanted nothing more than to lean in and kiss him - but she'd waited for so long, she didn't want it to happen under the shadow of what Sienna had done.

'Okay,' said Mike giving her a small nod and taking another swig of brandy. 'Anyway, it looks like I'm going to have to call Sarah's college in the morning and make sure they know what's what. It sounds like this plan got way further than it should have. There's no way I'm letting her miss out on something she's loving so much and is so good at just because her mother's a lunatic.'

'Good,' said Kate. 'Erm - do you think it might be a good idea to talk to the police . . . or maybe a solicitor?'

Mike frowned. 'I think I need to find out exactly what's happened - but yes, it might be time to put a few more barriers in place to stop this kind of thing from happening again.'

Kate was so tired, she almost felt drunk with it. It had taken her some serious convincing before Mike had agreed to her walking back to The Sardine alone the previous night. He was torn between wanting to make sure she got safely home and staying with Sarah. In the end, after Kate pointed out that it wasn't late and that she didn't have anything to fear from Sienna, he agreed to let her go provided that she called him the second she was back in her flat.

It had ended up being a restless night, and her dreams had been full of Sienna's angry face, and Mike's lips, and finally leaning in for the kiss that she now knew was about far more than simple, physical attraction.

She fired up the Italian Stallion for the second time in half an hour and poured herself a treacly triple espresso - it was the only way she was going to keep her eyes open today - and there was a lot to do.

Ethel and Charlie were driving over to the large theatre in Plymouth to pick up costumes for them all for the big day. They'd decided that there was no way they were going to let the side down - if Lee and Annabel wanted a wartime-themed wedding, that was what they were going to get - right down to the last victory roll.

Sarah was due in any minute - not to work a shift, but to get ready to meet with Annabel and Lee. It was time for her to show off her designs so that they could choose their final cake. In her heart, Kate knew that it wouldn't be the end of the world if Sarah decided that she simply wasn't up to it after yesterday - after all, both Lou and Ethel would no doubt be more than happy to step in if they needed to.

That wasn't the point though. Kate knew just how much this project meant to Sarah. She'd poured so much energy and passion into it. Plus, Kate had a sneaking suspicion that it was just what she needed to regain her confidence - as well as giving that bitch of a mother the middle finger.

Kate took a sip of her coffee and grimaced. Espresso was *so* not her drink - but it was definitely giving her the kind of jolt she needed to keep her on her feet. It really hadn't been late when she'd got back from Mike's, but the flat had been so quiet without Stanley there. She'd spent most of the night wishing she'd taken Mike up on his offer of sleeping in his spare room . . . but she hadn't dared to say yes.

From that moment their eyes had met on the sofa, Kate had been seconds away from crawling onto his lap and telling him that she'd fallen in love with him. One more sip of brandy and disaster would most definitely have struck! Okay - not disaster, but-

'Hey!'

The tinkle of the doorbell made her look up, only to find Paula grinning at her.

'Paula!' she said, rushing over and opening her arms for a hug. 'What brings you here so bright and early?'

'Well - two things,' she said, taking a step back. 'But first - why do you look like shit?'

'Gee thanks!' chuckled Kate, rolling her eyes. 'Just a rough night, that's all. Stanley had a sleepover with Sarah and I'm not used to him being away.'

'Aww!' said Paula. 'I can imagine. Okay - as long as you're not as ill as you look.'

'That might have something to do with the triple brandy I had with Mike,' sighed Kate.

'Oooh, Miss Hardy - is there gossip to share?'

'Nope,' said Kate. 'But almost. I nearly jumped on the poor guy!'

'Come on, Kate, what did we say about all this the other day?'

'I promise I'm working on it,' sighed Kate. 'But it's getting more complicated. Paula - I think I'm in love with him.'

'Holy shizzle sticks - the words I never thought I'd hear you say!' Paula grinned at her and jiggled excitedly on the spot. 'So . . . why not last night?'

'Bit of a long story,' muttered Kate, spotting a couple of people approaching the door, 'and not my story to tell,' she added in a whisper.

'Fairy snuff,' said Paula with a wink, sinking down into a chair and patting the table with her hands. 'Right, my hungover little turtle-dove. Back to *my* two things! Number one - scrambled eggs on toast and a latte pretty please!'

'You've got it!' said Kate with a smile.

'Number two - is Sarah here yet? She told me about her cake designs and I was hoping she might give me a sneaky peak.'

'She isn't, not yet. If I'm honest I'm not one hundred per cent sure that - oh!'

She'd just been about to tell Paula that she wasn't certain that they were going to see Sarah at all today when the teen in question bounced through the door and bounded right up to Kate.

'You are seriously the best and I love you,' she said, thrusting a bunch of flowers at Kate and then grabbing her in a massive cuddle.

Kate let out a delighted laugh and squeezed Sarah back with one arm, holding the flowers out to the side with the other to stop them from getting crushed. 'You okay, lovely?' she said quietly in her ear.

'Yes, thanks to you,' said Sarah. 'Sorry Paula,' she added, grinning over in her direction. 'Major drama with my bitch mother yesterday - she basically tried to kidnap me but Kate and Stanley saved me from a lifetime of servitude in Paris!'

The look of complete confusion on Paula's face made Kate giggle. 'Looks like I'll be able to share that story with you after all,' she said.

'Forget that - I'll tell it way better than you!' said Sarah, beaming at Paula.

'Erm, first - where's my dog?' said Kate.

'He's here,' said Mike, struggling into the cafe with a giant art portfolio under one arm, Stanley's lead looped over the other and a cardboard box precariously balanced in front of him. He plonked the box straight down on one of the tables and dropped Stanley's lead.

Stanley trotted up to Kate and she squatted down to bury her face in his fur. She'd really missed him - but that wasn't the only reason for the cuddle - he was the perfect way to distract herself from just how gorgeous Mike looked this morning - all pink-cheeked and flustered. Man, this was getting hard!

She could practically feel Paula's eyes boring into her back as she snuggled into Stanley, and she wasn't ready to meet her eyes until she'd got this blush under control!

'Careful with the box, dad!' squeaked Sarah, 'Jeez!'

Kate heard Mike laugh and peeped up at him. He was looking at his daughter with adoration, and suddenly she thought her heart was going to explode. She quickly got up and turned her back to make Paula's coffee.

'What *is* in the box?' asked Paula.

'It's one of the ideas I want to show Lee and Annabel!' said Sarah.

'Can I see?'

'Of course!' said Sarah. 'Kate - did you want to look too - I'd . . . erm . . . I'd really like to check you're happy with them before I take them over to the hotel and set them up for the others to look at. Dad says he likes them - but he *would* say that!'

'Sure,' said Kate over her shoulder. 'Give me two

secs.' She quickly poured the foamy milk into Paula's cup, then took it over to her as Sarah unzipped the massive portfolio and flipped the cover open.

'I've done three different ideas,' said Sarah. 'Only two of them are any good.'

Mike moved back so that Kate and Paula could see better, and as he did so, Kate's hand brushed the back of his. The tiny contact made all the hairs on the back of her neck stand on end.

Get a grip woman!

She stared down at the intricate drawings on the first page of the portfolio, doing her best to ignore Mike standing just behind her. If she leaned back just a little, she'd probably touch him.

'So!' said Sarah, sounding a bit nervous. 'This one's quite simple, but I wanted to go for that slightly "make-do-and-mend - everyone in it together" vibe where everyone might have given their rations to make it happen.'

The drawing showed a quirky take on the classic victoria sponge. There were the usual thick layers of jam and cream in the centre - but six layers made up three different cakes, all stacked on top of each other, angled slightly to give it a topsy-turvy look. The whole thing was finished off and decorated with piped cream and fresh strawberries.

'I know it's not exactly historically accurate - but I thought it had that quirky vintage-vibe,' said Sarah, now sounding decidedly nervous as all of them stared at the drawing in complete silence.

'Um - Sarah,' said Kate slowly, 'how come you never mentioned you could draw like this?!'

Sarah grinned at her and shrugged.

'Isn't it beautiful?' said Mike with a proud smile.

'I'd put that on my wall!' said Paula.

'Don't be silly,' said Sarah turning pink.

'I'm serious!' laughed Paula.

'But what about the cake?' whined Sarah.

'Perfect,' said Kate simply. 'It is beautiful. We've got a winner!'

'Hey - don't say that - you'll upset the other two!' laughed Sarah.

'Why do I get the feeling Lee and Annabel are going to end up with three wedding cakes, whether they want them or not?' chuckled Mike.

'Okay, next,' said Sarah flipping the page.

'Wow!' breathed Paula.

'I'm not sure about this one for the wedding, to be honest,' said Sarah, 'but I kinda needed to do this drawing for college so thought I might as well show them.'

This cake had the full VE day vibe - covered in little union jacks, poppies and Khaki piping details.

'It's so bold!' said Kate.

Sarah nodded. 'I had to show one with the theme - it's got vanilla and chocolate tiers too because I know they both love those flavours - but I don't think it's really *weddingy,* you know?'

'Okay, show us number three!' said Kate excitedly.

Sarah flipped the page to reveal drawings of ten different, exquisite cupcakes. 'These should work individually *and* give you a feel for the theme together,' she said.

Union Jack bunting, tiny fields of piped poppies, Vera Lyn lyrics, delicate creamy lace designs and many more all came together to create the perfect wartime vibe.

'You've just made this impossible to choose!' said Kate, shaking her head in wonder.

'They aren't the best bit!' said Sarah, her eyes sparkling. 'Pass me the box, dad!'

Mike grabbed the cardboard box and handed it over. Paula and Kate both leaned in, but Sarah kept her hand on the closed lid for a moment.

'Did you know that during the war and just after, because of rationing, the cake would often be just a small, simple fruitcake that friends and family would club together and pool their rations to make?'

'Not sure the happy couple want a tiny fruitcake though, love,' chuckled Mike.

'Not the point dad!' said Sarah, rolling her eyes. 'They used to make them look like fancy wedding cakes by creating a fake one out of cardboard and plaster that fitted over the top!'

She opened the box and drew out one of the most

beautiful cakes Kate had ever set eyes on. It was all creams and whites, with lace and pearls. The quintessential wedding cake - finished with little blue and white cameos on each tier.

'Wow!' said Paula.

'Yes, but . . .' Sarah flicked the edge of the cake with her finger and it made a hollow, thudding sound.

'Erm . . . what?!' said Kate.

'It's a wartime cake cover!' said Sarah with a grin. She quickly flipped to the next page in her portfolio. 'Instead of covering a tiny fruit cake, it's going to cover the cupcakes on a stand - and then they get revealed when Lee and Annabel come to "cut the cake!"' She grinned at them triumphantly. 'Do you think they'll like the ideas?' she suddenly added, her smile dropping.

Kate nodded. 'Definitely. These are absolutely beautiful - and seriously professional.'

'Thanks,' she said, breathing a sigh of relief. 'Erm . . . would it be okay if I go over to Pebble Street and set the pages out on the tables - just so it's easier to show them?'

Kate nodded. 'Of course, here . . .' she quickly rummaged in her handbag and drew out the front door key Lionel had given her.

'I'll help!' said Paula. 'You grab the portfolio, I'll bring the box. I'll grab my breakfast when we get back!' she grinned at Kate.

Mike and Kate watched the pair of them as they trooped back outside.

'Sarah seems to have bounced back well,' said Kate in wonder.

Mike nodded, giving her a weary smile. 'I've spoken to her tutors already. She was never unenrolled in the first place. Sienna's not down on their paperwork as Sarah's guardian - but the head of her course was going to contact me directly to find out what was going on. Apparently, they'd noticed that she was struggling with something.'

'So everything's okay?'

'It *will* be,' Mike nodded. 'We've had a good talk - and we will talk some more. Sienna's not coming anywhere near her for a very long time!' He paused and ruffled his hair awkwardly. 'Kate - I can't thank you . . . I don't know what would have happened if . . .'

He took a step towards her, and Kate swallowed as he reached out and took her hand.

'Kate, there's something we really need to talk about. I-'

The door of the cafe bashed open making Kate jump and quickly whip her hand away from Mike.

'What a to-do!' boomed Lionel, then he stopped dead, staring at them. 'Oh my, I'm terribly sorry!' he said with an awkward grin.

Kate shook her head and forced a smile at him.

'I'm just going to nip over and help Sarah,' said Mike, giving Kate a quick glance. 'We'll talk later?' he said and then quickly made a dash for the door.

As soon as it closed, Lionel looked back at her

sheepishly. 'I'm so sorry Kate - seems I interrupted at a bad moment?'

'Not at all,' said Kate briskly, doing her best to squash down the temptation to dash after Mike. 'You look rather worked up about something - everything okay?'

Lionel nodded and sighed. 'Only those duffers at the council up to their usual tricks,' he said.

'Uh oh, what ridiculous scheme have they come up with this time?'

Lionel grabbed the newspaper he had clamped under his arm and spread it out on the table, doing his best to iron out the creases.

Kate gasped as her eyes landed on the headline.

Seabury For Sale

'What do they mean, Seabury for Sale?' she demanded.

'They've gone and picked up on the story of Pebble Street being on the market,' said Lionel.

'But what were you saying about the council?' said Kate, trying to scan the article as fast as she could.

'In their wisdom, they've decided to sell off The King's Nose and-'

'Who'd want The King's Nose?' she huffed.

Lionel shrugged. 'Some developer or other, I guess. If they put a house on there, that'll more than ruin my view,' he sighed.

'Oh Lionel, they *wouldn't!*' she squeaked.

'Maybe,' he said. 'That's not all. They've put the old lighthouse on the market too.'

Kate felt like someone had just punched her in the gut, and she sank into the chair opposite him.

'I know. More change,' said Lionel sadly, but then he shook his head with a naughty grin. 'Typical of this rag to be behind the times as usual, though.'

'What do you mean?' said Kate weakly, not sure if she could take another ounce of bad news.

'The hotel's already sold!'

'Eh? Already?' said Kate, her surprise puncturing the fog of gloom that seemed to have suddenly descended.

'Yup,' said Lionel. 'I bought it.'

CHAPTER 18

Kate yanked the rack of costumes into place and looked around the breakfast lounge with her hands on her hips. She couldn't believe that the big day was finally here. She knew that she should be both excited about the afternoon to come, and proud of everything they'd achieved here at The Pebble Street Hotel - but all she felt right now was slightly sad and hollow.

Her whole life felt like it was up in the air. She knew that, in comparison to what Paula was going through, her problems were nothing. But with the future of The Sardine so uncertain, her best friend facing such a dark time and now, the lighthouse up for sale - well, putting a smile on her face to celebrate a wedding was proving to be far more difficult than she could have ever imagined.

Kate reached up to stroke a stray hair back into one

of her victory rolls and sighed. It was time for her to channel some of the bravery of the world war two wrens. She couldn't let the side down considering she was wearing their uniform. Today, she would put on the performance of a lifetime. She'd work the stiff upper lip and plaster a smile on her face. Starting now.

'Hello, beautiful - all ready?'

Paula's smiling face appeared at the doorway. 'Ooh look at it in here - it's perfect!' She beamed around, taking in the various dressing tables that had been added, complete with 1940s accessories, bobby pins, hair spray and anything else the wedding guests might require to fix their outfits throughout the day. 'I can't wait to see everyone in costume,' she sighed. 'Thank you so much for letting me be involved.'

'Are you kidding me?!' laughed Kate, going to stand beside her friend. 'We honestly couldn't have done this without you. And by the way - you look incredible!'

Paula was in costume too, her red lippy bringing some colour to her pale face.

'Hey - have you heard?' said Paula. 'Doreen and another one of WI girls have prepared a surprise for the happy couple.'

Kate raised her eyebrows. 'Uh oh,' she chuckled. 'I just hope Lee and Annabel won't regret inviting half of Seabury to their big day!'

'No chance,' said Paula, 'without half of Seabury, the day wouldn't be happening at all, would it?'

'Good point!' said Kate, and this time the smile that

spread across her face was genuine. 'So, is Ryan dressing up too?'

'You'd better believe it,' said Paula wiggling her eyebrows. 'Bet you can't wait to see Mike in uniform?'

Kate pulled a face. 'Actually, I . . . oh! Sorry!' her mobile had just started trilling. 'Better get this!' she muttered, not wanting to miss any kind of wedding related, last minute emergency.

'See you later!' whispered Paula, retreating out of the room.

'Kate speaking!' said Kate.

'Kate - it's Philip.'

A drop of ice-cold fear quickly dowsed her newly-found good mood. Her new solicitor calling her . . . on a Saturday?

'What's happened?' she gasped.

'Don't worry, it's good news,' said Philip quickly. 'I'm sorry to call, I know you're busy today - Lionel told me about the wedding - but I knew you wouldn't want to wait a second longer than necessary.'

Good news? He'd just said good news, right?

'Kate - it's all over. The Sardine's safe. Tom is dropping all further claims.'

'Wait,' she breathed, her heart hammering, 'what?!'

'No court case. No having to sell the cafe. Oh, and you're to stop paying your spousal payments immediately.'

Kate grasped the back of the chair in front of her with her free hand for support.

'But - how?! I don't understand?!'

'We'll go through all the nitty-gritty next week. I've got some paperwork for you to sign as long as you're happy with everything. But it'll mean a clean break and your divorce will be finalised without delay.'

'I think I love you!' said Kate, barely able to contain herself.

She heard Philip chuckle.

'Sorry, sorry!' said Kate quickly. 'This is just . . . I . . . *thank you!*'

'It's very much my pleasure,' he said earnestly. 'It turns out that Tom is engaged to be married. Plus, his new partner is pregnant. I'm afraid he had some rather outlandish ideas about you funding his new life.'

'*What?!*' gasped Kate.

'Yes. As Lionel said to me the other day - despicable. But you're free, Miss Hardy, and - most importantly - The Sardine is safe.'

'I don't know how to thank you,' breathed Kate, barely daring to believe what he was telling her.

'Well, Lionel tells me you do the most exquisite cakes?' he chuckled.

'You're on free cake boxes for life!' laughed Kate.

'All the best with the wedding, Miss Hardy. And I look forward to meeting with you next week to finalise everything.'

Kate slipped her mobile back into her pocket, then grasped the chair with both hands and squeezed hard, watching her knuckles turn white. She wasn't asleep. This wasn't a dream. The Sardine was safe.

Taking in a deep breath, she squeezed her eyes closed and let out a loud squeal.

'Kate?!'

She whirled around to find a soldier standing framed in the doorway.

Kate went completely still. She couldn't say a word, but she let out a breathy little gasp as she took in the cap sitting on his perfectly swept-back hair, then her eyes travelled down to his neat khaki shirt and perfectly polished boots. She opened her mouth to speak but she still couldn't make a sound.

'What's the matter?' said Mike, not taking his eyes off of her as he took a step into the room.

'I . . . you . . .'

'Are you okay? I thought I heard you scream or something?'

She nodded quickly, watching as Mike fiddled awkwardly with his cuffs.

'I . . .'

The Sardine was safe and Mike was here. This wonderful man she'd completely fallen for. What on earth was she waiting for?

Something inside her snapped. Letting go of the chair, she flew towards him and jumped. Mike's arms wrapped around her instinctively, lifting her against him as her lips found his, even as their combined weight made him stumble backwards, out into the hallway.

'Get a room, you two!' came Sarah's delighted squeal.

Kate could feel Mike chuckle even before her lips left his. Without letting go of him, she turned her head only to find Paula, Lou, Sarah and Ethel watching them with matching Cheshire-cat grins on their faces.

Stanley trotted up to the pair of them and wound around Mike's legs, excitedly wagging his tail. Mike still had his arms wrapped around Kate, holding her entire weight up off the floor as she clung to him.

'So romantic!' sighed Lou.

'Eew!' laughed Sarah, though it was clear by the look on her face she was thrilled. 'What got into you crazy kids?!'

'The Sardine's safe!' said Kate quickly, unable to keep the huge grin off of her face.

'What?!' said Mike.

'Oh my goodness! This is the most wonderful news,' said Ethel, grabbing Sarah's hand and jumping up and down on the spot.

Mike turned back to Kate with a smile and Kate stared at him, losing herself in his beautiful eyes, and for a moment it was as if everything else faded into the background.

'Erm . . . we've got a wedding to run here, guys!' laughed Paula.

'It'll wait a moment,' said Mike not taking his eyes

off of Kate, and then, totally ignoring the fact that they now had an audience, he leaned in and kissed her again.

Kate leaned back against the makeshift bar in the corner of the dining room and watched as Lee led Annabel out into the middle of the floor for their first dance. The band struck up an old Glenn Miller favourite, and the handsome soldier drew his beautiful bride into the slowest of slow dances.

Kate turned to watch the band with tears in her eyes. Who'd have thought they'd be so amazing?

'Just about perfect,' said Paula, snagging a glass of bubbly from behind the bar as she joined her. Kate nodded and leaned her head on Paula's shoulder.

The room really was just about perfect. There were flowers everywhere - the old-fashioned kind that looked like they came from a cottage garden - and bunting and union jacks looped across the ceiling. Trixie had started proceedings in pride of place in the centre of the room - but now that everyone had eaten their fill, she'd been moved off to the side to make room for the dancing. Kate would need to move her out to the kitchen shortly to load up Sarah's stunning cake - ready for its grand entrance. The pair had opted for the monumental Victoria sponge, and Ethel had sourced a whole load of vintage side-plates and cake forks so that the guests would be able to help themselves in style.

'Ladies!' said Lionel, coming over to them, taking his cap off and giving them a little bow. He looked every inch the proud soldier in his uniform.

'Not a bad house-warming party, eh Lionel?' chuckled Paula.

He smiled warmly at her. 'Watch this space, my dear. I've got a feeling this is just the first of many.'

Kate let out a happy sigh, watching as other couples started to join Lee and Annabel on the dance floor. She could just about make out Stanley over the other side of the room. He was wearing his own miniature soldier's cap that Doreen had made for him, and he looked like he was in his element. Guests had been taking it in turns to feed him titbits and take selfies with him all night.

'May I have this dance?' said Ryan, coming up and holding his hand out to Paula.

'You've got it!' said Paula, giving Kate a quick peck on the cheek before disappearing out onto the dance floor.

'Aw, look at old Charlie,' said Kate, as she watched him lead Ethel proudly into position.

'I wouldn't be surprised if theirs is the next shindig we hold here,' chuckled Lionel.

Kate beamed. 'Imagine that!' she said. 'I'm so happy that this place is in your safe hands.'

'I've got big plans,' said Lionel, 'but there's plenty of

time to fill you in on all that. Looks like you've got more important things coming your way,' he wiggled his eyebrows at her as Mike drew near.

'Slacking, are we?' grinned Mike.

Kate blushed. 'Just for a moment, yes!'

'Well, time to put that drink down, Miss Hardy.'

Kate groaned. 'Why, what's up?'

'Absolutely nothing! But if Lionel can spare you for a moment, may I have this dance?' he asked, holding out his hand.

Kate smiled shyly at him and then let him lead her onto the floor, only for the song to come to an end the minute they started to dance.

'Awkward,' chuckled Mike and they turned towards the band to clap with everyone else. 'Erm - what's Sarah up to?'

She was carrying an old fashioned silver microphone on a stand and set it down right next to the trumpet player.

'We've got a surprise for Lee and Annabel,' she said shyly, her voice coming through loud and clear. 'I'd like to welcome to the stage ... Doreen and Celia!'

There was a scattering of confused clapping as the pair of them, their matching victory rolls and red lippy still perfectly in place, took up position behind the microphone.

Kate let out a gasp as, without another word, the band struck up a slow number and Doreen launched into the Vera Lynn wartime classic, *We'll Meet Again*.

'Oh my goodness,' breathed Kate, as Celia's voice joined her friend's in perfect harmony. She glanced over at Annabel and watched as Lee drew out his handkerchief and dabbed at the happy tears that were now trickling down her face.

'Just about perfect,' whispered Mike.

Kate nodded with a sigh and turned back to him, only to find his eyes on hers.

The cool evening breeze felt wonderful against her hot face, and Kate sucked in a long breath of sea air.

'Here,' said Mike, handing her a fresh glass of bubbly.

'Thank you,' said Kate gratefully. 'And here's to it all going without a hitch,' she added, clinking her glass against his and smiling as the music drifted out of the dining room behind them.

'Not too bad for a first attempt,' said Mike with a smile, then shyly reaching down, he stroked a stray hair back from her cheek. 'Almost perfect.'

'Almost,' she said, unable to stop her eyes from straying over towards the lighthouse.

'Kate?'

'Hm?'

'Remember the other day I said there was something we needed to talk about?'

'Erm . . . not really!' said Kate with a sheepish smile

as she turned back to him. 'Sorry - there's been so much going on.'

'Yeah,' said Mike. 'There has . . .'

Kate raised her eyebrows. It was strange to see Mike looking so nervous. 'What's up, soldier?' she said, giving him a cheeky wink.

Mike took her hand and Kate's heart did a somersault as he kissed the back of it.

'I . . . well . . . the lighthouse . . .'

'Oh!' said Kate in surprise.

'I know how you must be feeling, but-'

'DAD!'

They both turned to find Sarah standing in the doorway of the dining room.

'What's up?' called Mike, a slightly dazed look on his face.

'Can you help? One of the strings of bunting just came down and nearly garrotted everyone,' she laughed.

Mike rolled his eyes and glanced at Kate. 'I'll be right back!'

Kate smiled and nodded, watching as he disappeared inside to help Sarah.

'Hi!'

Kate jumped as one of the wedding guests appeared next to her.

'Oops, sorry, I didn't think you'd spotted me!' she laughed, patting her hair and taking a swig from her glass. 'I just wanted to say thank you for making this such a special night.'

'Oh,' said Kate, beaming at her, 'it's been our pleasure.'

'Well, I hope you're ready for lots more events!' she laughed. 'I work for one of the estate agents over in Plymouth, and trust me - you're getting *all* the corporate events from now on!'

'Well, erm . . . gosh!' said Kate, slightly taken aback. 'This was our first one, just to test things out - you know?'

'Yes,' she said, raising her eyebrows. 'But I assumed that, as you're purchasing a premises, you'll be going great guns!'

'Premises?' said Kate, shaking her head in confusion.

'Yes!' laughed the woman. 'You *are* the other half of Frothy Sardine, right?'

'Well, I . . . erm . . .'

Kate's mind was racing. What the hell was going on here?'

'I mean, you guys have bought the old lighthouse . . . so?'

'Lighthouse? The lighthouse? I . . . I'm sorry, I . . .'

'Mike!' said the woman, turning to greet him as he strode back outside. 'I think your partner might have had enough bubbly,' she giggled. 'Congratulations again on buying the old place. I *know* you're going to love it.'

'Mike?' breathed Kate. Her heart was hammering,

and the hairs on the back of her neck were prickling. 'Frothy Sardine? The Lighthouse? What's she talking about.'

'I've been trying to talk to you for days,' said Mike, looking freaked.

Kate raised her eyebrows, unable to say a word. He came to stand right in front of her and took both of her hands in his.

'Look - there's no other way to put this. I'm in love with you.'

Kate's mouth dropped open. She wanted to tell him that she was in love with him too. That she really and truly had *never* felt like this before. But she couldn't get the words out.

'Kate,' said Mike, squeezing her hands lightly. 'I bought the lighthouse.'

THE END

Kate and Stanley's story concludes with
Christmas in Seabury

ALSO BY BETH RAIN

Seabury Series:

Welcome to Seabury (Seabury Book 1)

Trouble in Seabury (Seabury Book 2)

Christmas in Seabury (Seabury Book 3)

Sandwiches in Seabury (Seabury Book 4)

Secrets in Seabury (Seabury Book 5)

Surprises in Seabury (Seabury Book 6)

Dreams and Ice Creams in Seabury (Seabury Book 7)

Mistakes and Heartbreaks in Seabury (Seabury Book 8)

Laughter and Happy Ever After in Seabury (Seabury Book 9)

A Quiet Life in Seabury (Seabury Book 10)

In A Spin in Seabury (Seabury Book 11)

Living The Dream in Seabury (Seabury Book 12)

A Big Day in Seabury (Seabury Book 13)

Something Borrowed in Seabury (Seabury Book 14)

A Match Made in Seabury (Seabury Book 15)

Seabury Series Collections:

Kate's Story: Books 1 - 3

Hattie's Story: Books 4 - 6

Standalones: Books 7 - 9

Lizzie's Story: Books 10 - 12

Upper Bamton Series:

Upper Bamton: The Complete Series Collection: Books 1 - 4

Individual titles:

A New Arrival in Upper Bamton (Upper Bamton Book 1)

Rainy Days in Upper Bamton (Upper Bamton Book 2)

Hidden Treasures in Upper Bamton (Upper Bamton Book 3)

Time Flies By in Upper Bamton (Upper Bamton Book 4)

Standalone Books:

How to be Angry at Christmas

Crumbleton Series:

Coming Home to Crumbleton (Crumbleton Book 1)

Flowers Go Flying in Crumbleton (Crumbleton Book 2)

Match Point in Crumbleton (Crumbleton Book 3)

A Very Crumbleton Christmas (Crumbleton Book 4)

Little Bamton Series:

Little Bamton: The Complete Series Collection: Books 1 - 5

Individual titles:

Christmas Lights and Snowball Fights (Little Bamton Book 1)

Spring Flowers and April Showers (Little Bamton Book 2)

Summer Nights and Pillow Fights (Little Bamton Book 3)

Autumn Cuddles and Muddy Puddles (Little Bamton Book 4)

Christmas Flings and Wedding Rings (Little Bamton Book 5)

Crumcarey Island Series:

Crumcarey Island Series Collection: Books 1 - 5

Individual titles:

Christmas on Crumcarey (Crumcarey Island Book 1)

All Change on Crumcarey (Crumcarey Island Book 2)

Making Waves on Crumcarey (Crumcarey Island Book 3)

Fool's Gold on Crumcarey (Crumcarey Island Book 4)

A Fresh Start on Crumcarey (Crumcarey Island Book 5)

WRITING AS BEA FOX

What's a Girl To Do? The Complete Series

Individual titles:

The Holiday: What's a Girl To Do? (Book 1)

The Wedding: What's a Girl To Do? (Book 2)

The Lookalike: What's a Girl To Do? (Book 3)

The Reunion: What's a Girl To Do? (Book 4)

At Christmas: What's a Girl To Do? (Book 5)

ABOUT THE AUTHOR

Beth Rain has always wanted to be a writer and has been penning adventures for characters ever since she learned to stare into the middle-distance and daydream.

She recently moved to a windswept, Scottish island, and it is a dream come true to spend her days hanging out with Bob – her trusty laptop – scoffing crisps and chocolate while dreaming up swoony love stories for all her imaginary friends.

Beth's writing will always deliver on the happy-ever-afters, so if you need cosy… you're in safe hands!

Visit www.bethrain.com for all the bookish goodness and keep up with all Beth's news by joining her newsletter!

facebook.com/BethRainBooks
twitter.com/bethrainauthor
instagram.com/bethrainauthor

Printed in Dunstable, United Kingdom